Pa... let go of the ladder and dropped agilely onto the chest of one of the fresh government corpses. Without thought, as he threw himself away from the body, he snatched the .357 from his waistband, aimed, and was squeezing the trigger before he was able to check the reaction. He froze where he was, poised on the balls of his feet, with one hand pressed against the pavement for support, and tried to make sense of what he beheld.

He'd encountered enough brand-new stiffs over the years to know them when he saw them. Two more deaths would now be added to his bogus list of victims.

Someone had killed to keep him free again—a jealous presence with whom he shared the night.

Other Action-Packed Adventures
*in the **ROGUE AGENT** Series*
from Avon Books

(#1) ROGUE AGENT
(#2) HARD TO KILL

Coming Soon

(#4) LAST RITES

Avon Books are available at special quantity discounts for bulk purchases for sales promotions, premiums, fund raising or educational use. Special books, or book excerpts, can also be created to fit specific needs.

For details write or telephone the office of the Director of Special Markets, Avon Books, Dept. FP, 105 Madison Avenue, New York, New York 10016, 212-481-5653.

BLOOD MONEY

JACK DRAKE

AVON BOOKS • NEW YORK

ROGUE AGENT #3: BLOOD MONEY is an original publication of Avon Books. This work has never before appeared in book form. This work is a novel. Any similarity to actual persons or events is purely coincidental.

AVON BOOKS
A division of
The Hearst Corporation
105 Madison Avenue
New York, New York 10016

Copyright © 1991 by Bruce King
Last Rites excerpt copyright © 1991 by Bruce King
Published by arrangement with the author
Library of Congress Catalog Card Number: 90-93606
ISBN: 0-380-76177-7

All rights reserved, which includes the right to reproduce this book or portions thereof in any form whatsoever except as provided by the U.S. Copyright Law. For information address Richard Curtis Associates, 164 East 64th Street, New York, New York 10021.

First Avon Books Printing: May 1991

AVON TRADEMARK REG. U.S. PAT. OFF. AND IN OTHER COUNTRIES, MARCA REGISTRADA, HECHO EN U.S.A.

Printed in the U.S.A.

RAI 10 9 8 7 6 5 4 3 2 1

For Dean R. Koontz

whose sage advice has contributed
greatly to whatever this writer
does that is of some worth

1

It was the flight crew who alerted Paine that he'd been made. Civilians were no good at keeping secrets.

They weren't obvious about it. Not, at least, as such things were measured outside the game. But from John Paine's perspective, they might as well have carried signs.

Somewhere between Ireland and Iceland, their opinion of him changed. For the worse. The two female flight attendants and one male who'd occasionally been making eyes at him stopped doing so. Paine sensed there were more brief, whispered consultations among them than normal.

Small things. Nuances. But such small warnings were usually all you got. And then, only if you were paying attention. Paine had been paying attention for a long time. Since his violent and patriotic youth. As a field agent for the Central Intelligence Agency, it was his profession. By extension, it was all he knew, and the reason he was still alive and free.

From one side of the Atlantic or the other, a message had been sent. A mistake on someone's part for which Paine was grateful.

One of your passengers, a large man who currently goes by the name of Alan Nolan, is a renegade spy. He is a trained killer who is wanted for murder in Switzerland, England, and France. He is also suspected of treason in his native land. The United States government will be throwing a surprise party for him when he arrives. Be advised it is a private party that your crew and passengers would do well to avoid. Since the reception committee is bringing guns, it could be rather loud. In view of "Mr. Nolan's" historic response to similar situations, there is also a strong chance that it will be quite bloody.

Paine wondered how he'd given himself away. The Nolan identity had been a virgin when he'd assumed it in Paris. The progress of the documents he'd prepared—from the trunk in Cunningham's basement, through his trusted friend's expert hands, to the international carrier, and finally to him at the pickup point—had been without apparent flaw. It should have carried him much further than it had.

It must have been the rental car he'd dumped in Saint-Malo. He'd left it in a place where it should have been overlooked for days, but he hadn't hidden it as effectively as he would have if he'd had more time. It was hard to be neat when every cop on the Continent was breathing down your neck.

Paine used the remaining flight time to chart a course for himself in the days that lay ahead. The first item on the agenda was how best to keep the civilian body count to a minimum when they touched down at Kennedy. There were times, he knew, when friendly casualties could not be avoided. In his experience, warfare seldom erupted in places, and at times, when it was most convenient. It simply happened when opposing forces came together, wherever and whenever that might be. Sometimes that was in the far corner of nowhere at 2:00 A.M. Other times it was Piccadilly Circus during rush hour or St. Peter's Square on Christmas Eve.

A man took what fate handed him and made the best of what was often a disaster from the start. But Paine already had more dead bystanders behind him than he cared to contemplate. He was not looking forward to seeing that roster lengthen appreciably in the first few minutes after the 747 landed.

Not that he had any interest in dying in order to show the world that he was, down deep, a nice person. Paine was not a nice person, no matter how deeply one might explore. He knew that, and was not troubled by the knowledge. He knew that a lot of other people knew it, too. That didn't trouble him either. He didn't care what happened to the Amazon rain forest. *He* was the only animal whose possible extinction made him sweat from time to time.

Nonetheless, the prospect of innocents being butchered in bunches on his account revolted the vestiges of his humanity.

It was 9:47 P.M. of a July Thursday when the landing gear dropped into position beneath John Paine's feet. Homecoming. He didn't need a window to see the way they had it all arranged. *They*. His comrades. His countrymen. The Company. The FBI, as well, now, more than likely.

There would be no massed troops; no weapons in the open; no uniforms. Not, at least, where any of the voting public could see them. He had become a severe embarrassment, dirty laundry that had to be washed in front of an audience. They would do their utmost to keep his "maximal demotion" as contained and deniable as possible.

There was only one small problem. Unless one counted Paine's fondness for staying alive. That made two. The other was the fact that those who sought to neutralize him now were the same ones who had trained him, or clones of the ones who had. And they were almost as good at teaching as he was at learning.

Paine had been the man in charge of more than one such operation himself in recent years. They would be following a manual of procedures to which he had been a major contributor. Paine was darkly pleased at the certainty that this made some of those who were now his enemies distinctly uncomfortable.

Including the mole. Whoever that might be.

That was the reason for his return. He'd been a player for too long to remain on the sidelines thousands of miles away, letting the game be decided by default. Allowing a cunning traitor to continue pulling his strings from the shadows. A puppet master who laughed behind a mask while he made Paine and the Company and the country look like circus clowns.

So far the mole was way out ahead on points. The Continent and the United Kingdom were littered with agents who'd been turned into stiffs or stooges by someone inside the Company who was engaged in sabotage of the worst kind. There was no other worthy explanation for one blown operation after another, starting with the homicidal farce that exploded around Paine in East Germany. The one that left Wilson, another Company man, dead by his own hand after his failed attempt to terminate Paine for a reason that Paine still could not comprehend.

Things didn't get that fouled up without serious help from someone. Whoever it was wanted Paine dead or running loose with a reputation as a traitor preceding him wherever he went like the din of a leper's bell, alerting everyone in his path to have a deadly welcome ready when he arrived.

The mole hadn't yet succeeded in getting him killed, but Paine had been driven so far out into the cold that the North Pole looked downright balmy by comparison. It was no place to be if you were a spy, a deadly climate where you had no friends, no safe harbors, and nothing but your survival skills to keep you from freezing solid.

The impact of the jumbo's vast weight slamming back down to earth was only reduced by the clusters of tires and shock absorbers, not eliminated. Paine could feel the tremors from the soles of his shoes all the way to his molars. Then the air brakes kicked in, and whatever else they used to keep the winged warehouse out of Jamaica Bay. Paine found the sudden, drastic deceleration disturbing, as usual. He had a profound distrust of landings. Given his choice, he would have preferred jumping as the plane passed over the field. So long as he had packed the chute himself.

Paine released his seat belt, preparing to move before the 747 reached the end of the runway. He had not returned to America simply to be killed on native soil, or captured, which would amount to the same thing since a stationary target was easier to hit, and there were those who would be only too happy to take advantage of that opportunity.

He was back because he was tired of running. It went against his nature and his training to remain for very long on the defensive. It was time to light a fire under the opposition; to get in close and harry them; to make *them* worry and lose sleep...for a change.

The passengers in the surrounding seats eyed him anxiously when he rose silently and moved into the aisle with the air of a man who knew what he was doing and was confident that it was altogether proper. In reality, John Paine wasn't quite sure what he was doing. Neither did he give a damn about its propriety. He had learned, however, that it was helpful in his line of work to always give the impression that you knew what you were up to and were sensitive to its appropriateness.

It kept people calm and out of your way.

"Sir!" A flight attendant called to him tentatively from somewhere to his rear. It didn't sound like her heart was really in it. Paine assumed both that she knew he was the turncoat serial killer they'd been warned about and that it was a conditioned response that she was helpless to prevent. Passenger strolls when the craft was taxiing were strictly *verboten*. Everyone knew that.

Paine ignored her, smiling and nodding reassuringly at everyone in general as he made his way toward the emergency exit he had selected for deplaning slightly ahead of schedule. He had already targeted the men between his seat and the hatch who were potential problems. The first one who even looked froggy would get a crash course in self-restraint that would convince the rest that cowardice was not always a vice.

"I beg your pardon!" The matron in the aisle seat of the row leading to the exit addressed herself to Paine with practiced indignation.

"Think nothing of it," Paine replied. When he was sure he had the attention of the other four occupants of the seats between him and the bulkhead, he said, "I'm on my way to the emergency exit at the end of this row. That may sound like a crazy proposition to some of you, but you have my word I am not a lunatic. I am, however, in a big hurry and dead set on getting my way. We can do this the easy way or the hard way. The easy way is for all of you to get out of my way and make yourselves as small as you can arrange. Anything else will be the hard way, and it will get you hurt. Which will it be?" Paine let them know with his body language that they would not have time for lengthy deliberation.

He looked down at the matron, who appeared to be waiting for someone in a position of authority to race to her rescue.

He dropped the warmth and reassurance. "I'm a desperate man, lady. Move it or lose it."

She moved it. As Paine advanced between the seats, the others followed her example.

"This must be your idea of a really inventive suicide." The woman who spoke was seated next to the exit. She impressed Paine as an executive in her dress-for-success business suit. She had a good face, confident and smart, and the sort of blue eyes that he favored.

As he got a solid, two-handed grip on the exit's operating lever, Paine made a quick survey of the cabin. He noted one of the attendants hurrying away toward the cockpit. The cockpit, where the radio was located. His welcoming committee would learn in a matter of seconds that their quarry was on the move.

"We must still be doing fifty miles per hour. Maybe sixty," the brunette huddled next to him said.

Paine had to exert considerable strength to get the lever to rotate. He found that reassuring. For years he had wondered how easily someone might pop one at thirty thousand feet. "That sounds like an accurate guess to me," he responded, glancing at her amused expression for several seconds, finding her more appealing the longer he looked at her. "To the contrary, I'm hoping this is a really inventive way to survive. One way or the other, I should have an answer very soon now."

Suddenly the rotating lever activated alarms

throughout the aircraft. Crash lights blazed to life all around Paine. Over every seat a compartment opened to drop an oxygen tube with mask attached in front of each passenger, like a sudden invasion of transparent spiders.

"You sure know how to make a boffo first impression," the woman said with a dry wit that Paine found impressive under the circumstances.

"So I've been told," he responded, concentrating on the feel and sound of the locks releasing around the hatch.

"Let's hope the next impression you make isn't in the surface of the runway," the woman added.

"It's kind of you to care," Paine replied, fixing his eyes on hers as he braced himself for what came next.

"Think nothing of it," she said, holding his gaze, "but if you hit the ground running, it's 313-4917. I could do with a little excitement. Think you can remember that?"

"No sweat," Paine answered, with a bemused expression and an elevated brow. "I have a mind like a mousetrap."

"Just my type," she said with a smile. "No challenge."

Paine didn't know how much force was required. To be on the safe side, he gave the hatch a very hard shove. He was so successful that he nearly left the plane with it before he could let go.

He caught himself with both hands on the fuselage, and his upper half suddenly bathed in a swift passing flow of the sultry New York summer night. Three stories below, the concrete was a racing gray river that reflected the brilliance of a score of landing lights.

A veteran of several hundred jumps, most of which had been made under conditions that could be classified starting at "perilous" and ending at "dead on arrival," John Paine was unimpressed by the physical risk involved. Nonetheless, he was pleased to see the emergency escape ramp deploying beneath him, bursting from its compartment in the fuselage beneath the exit. In seconds it inflated like a long orange tongue, extending from his perch all the way down to the ground, or very close to it.

As he pulled his legs through the hatch, it occurred to Paine that the plane seemed to be spitting out one of its passengers whom it found tasteless and indigestible. He let himself drop onto the slippery slide, folding his arms over his chest, keeping his feet together, pointing his toes at the uprushing concrete. The metaphor served well. He'd been getting that sort of treatment by assorted individuals, organizations, and sovereign states for several weeks now. He was sorely tired of it.

Tired of being persona non grata. Framed. Hunted. Marked for termination.

More than tired. Enraged. Violent. Homicidal.

Paine found his fury very useful when he flew off the end of the ramp, tucked and rolled, let his big body execute one complete revolution before spread-eagling onto his back. He stayed that way only long enough for his momentum to slow to the point where he could gain his feet and run.

As he sprinted toward the airport's perimeter, Paine did not look back. There was a line of 727s in front of him through which he had to pass. Without being parboiled by their exhaust or squashed beneath their wheels as they taxied toward takeoff. Thus, he did not see the other passenger who bailed out of the jumbo just as he had moments before. His pursuer was smaller and more agile than Paine, a lithe form that dove through the exit and slithered down the ramp like an otter descending a wet bank into a stream.

The figure hit the runway with balletic grace, and darted toward Paine's diminishing silhouette.

"Suspect is probably armed and is extremely dangerous. Paine is six four, two hundred thirty pounds, and in excellent condition."

Port Authority patrolman Salvatore Bonaventre listened intently to the alert being broadcast through his walkie-talkie. Unconsciously he flipped his chewing gum from one side of his mouth to the other as he nodded his head resolutely. Bonaventre hoped he'd get a shot at bagging the desperado. It would be a chance to prove to his supervisor that he was too good a man to be stuck walking patrol on the stinking boundary of Kennedy forever.

"He is forty-four with a gray crewcut." Bonaventre ignored the remainder of the physical description. The bad guy wouldn't be hard to spot if he came within range. He'd be the only other swinging dick in the vicinity. It would be just the two of them. *Mano a mano*. Bonaventre smiled grimly. That would be fine with him. Size and strength didn't worry him. He had both himself.

"Approach suspect with caution. Do not, repeat, do *not* attempt to apprehend without assistance. If he resists, *shoot him*. Your judgment will not be questioned. This authorization comes from the very highest level." Bonaventre frowned at that. He wondered what was going on. He'd never imagined that he might be told to waste somebody if they didn't cooperate. That didn't sound like solid police procedure to him, regardless of what this Paine might have done.

John Paine froze twenty feet behind the patrolman when Bonaventre seemed about to turn around. Paine kept his breathing shallow and through his mouth. All his weight was balanced on the balls of his feet. The surrounding area was brightly illuminated and devoid of cover. He had only speed and silence and the distraction of the radio to depend on.

Like a stalking tiger, he maintained his pose until he was sure his prey had not sensed his approach. Then he took another step forward, and another. The distant whine of jet engines cloaked the small sounds of his advance.

Paine was not surprised by the orders the young officer received. He was not a common criminal, and he did not expect to be granted the consideration that such a man could expect. If he was a criminal at all, Paine liked to think that he was most uncommon, and could take care of himself without any assistance from the Bill of Rights.

When he took Bonaventre, he did it as he had done it to scores of sentries over the years, going all the way back to the war, when his opponents were comparatively small and their necks were broken with ease. He locked the big kid's jaw in the vise of his left arm, and yanked his head back, pulling him off balance with the broad back arched and trapped against his chest. That was a killing posture, with Bonaventre's vulnerable throat exposed.

But Paine had neither the desire nor the need to take the patrolman's life.

"You're out of your league" were the last sounds Sal would hear for a while. With wide, frightened eyes, he fought to breathe as Paine's hard right hand seized his throat, the first two fingers and thumb jammed into the yielding flesh on either side of his larynx, shutting down the carotids that supplied oxygen to his brain, putting him to sleep, but maintaining the pressure only long enough for that. It was a dicey technique that could result in a major reduction in the subject's IQ if applied too zealously, but Paine knew how to apply it with finesse.

Bonaventre regained consciousness ten minutes later in his underwear with his wrists locked together behind his back and connected to his bound ankles with the ligature of a dress shirt purchased recently on the Champs Elysées.

He understood why the orders he'd been given were so drastic.

And he knew with depressing certainty that he could look forward to a lot more time walking patrol on the perimeter.

But only if he was lucky.

2

"Marvelous. Superb. Impeccable. A truly brain-dead performance on the part of all concerned." Lucian Brock, the Director of the Central Intelligence Agency, sat behind his desk, looking through the glass wall of his office at the lush Virginia countryside. The manicured nails of his right hand shone in the light as he tapped his fingers rhythmically on the polished mahogany. "We get Paine handed to us on a plate by some helpful anonymous informant, right in our own backyard, and he gives my best troops the slip like a bunch of rookies standing around playing pocket-pool." Brock exhaled forcefully, but kept his voice low and his delivery measured. He acted like a man who was used to wielding great authority and getting results when he issued orders.

The two men on the other side of the desk knew that Brock was just that. They said nothing. Both were thinking over the various career options open to "retired" spy managers, should the need arise, in the next few painful minutes, to pursue them.

"This entire fiasco is gaining momentum by the day," Brock continued. "It is already out of control. This Agency cannot afford any bad publicity. Not now. Not when I am spending most of my time on the Hill, kissing all the congressional ass I can find, in pursuit of a bigger budget." He turned from the window to vivisect the two men with his eyes. "I will not have one operative who has broken his leash looking like he is the equal of our entire organization. Do I make myself clear?"

Both men nodded silently. Mark Berghold, the head of Internal Security for the Company, was ten years younger than the other two. He otherwise resembled them in most respects, a trim middle-aged executive in a conservative three-piece suit. He had been the man ultimately responsible for Paine's reception at Kennedy International the night before. If anyone would get the ax for the operation's failure, he was the most likely and logical candidate.

He had been around long enough to know better than to make any attempt at his own defense. The fact was, he had underestimated John Paine's resourcefulness, audacity, and ability to smell even a whiff of danger on the wind. Berghold was beginning to understand that Paine was a breed apart. The handful of men like Paine who worked for the Company were as different from the standard field operative as the standard field operative was from the average civilian. They weren't "organization men." They were chosen for their roles as roving, independent troubleshooters because they functioned best outside the system.

Having such a man go bad on them was the sort of disaster all three had hoped they would never have to face. Now that it was upon them, it was becoming more obvious all the time how justified their fears had been concerning it. Paine was better than anyone they sent against him. Smarter, tougher, more experienced. Worst of all, Berghold realized, Paine was unorthodox and creative in his approach to problems. As a result, it was nearly impossible to anticipate his next move. That was what made him such a lethal weapon in the field. The enemy could never predict his plans; could neither mount an effective defense nor an effective attack against him.

Unfortunately, the Company had become the enemy. In the beginning, when Wilson died, either with or without help from John Paine, it had seemed important to determine which side, or sides, Paine was really on. But the situation had deteriorated so badly since then that the question of his allegiance had become academic. For whatever reasons, Paine had declared war on his former employers.

Bill Mitchell had payed with his life in Paris for trying too hard to bring Paine in. Morgan Hill, another sanction specialist like Paine, had very nearly done the same in London when Paine decided to get between him and a target.

Paine was no longer answering to anyone but himself. For all practical purposes, he was a deserter. And since hostilities had never ceased among the nations in the arena of espionage,

Paine had deserted in time of war. Every commander knew the sole penalty for that crime, as did his troops.

Summary execution.

The problem was that passing sentence on certain men was much easier than seeing to it that the judgment was carried out.

With the previous night's humiliation and Brock's open contempt eating like acid at his pride, Mark Berghold was ready to do whatever it took to bring the renegade down. If necessary, he would go outside normal channels and hire a "contract agent," a professional killer who would be more on a par with Paine himself.

After all, Berghold reasoned, if Paine saw no need to play by the rules, why should the Company hobble itself by continuing to observe them?

"You've had some time to look into this mess, George," Brock said to the other man seated across from him. "What have you come up with?"

George Rafferty, the DCI's unofficial second-in-command and able right hand, sat forward in his chair, preparing to make his presentation.

"That's right, Lucian. About eight hours, to be exact. Until the situation went critical at Kennedy last night—" Rafferty cast a frigid glance in Berghold's direction—"I assumed we had the problem fairly well contained. Since then, in lieu of sleep, I've been shaking every tree in sight, collecting all the information I could find about who we're dealing with." Rafferty opened the manila folder he'd been holding in his lap, and started flipping through the pages it contained.

Rafferty was the master of all the hard intelligence that passed through Langley. He was reputed to have something akin to an unnatural relationship with "Octopus," the monstrous computer that was the storehouse of all data, from the crucial to the insignificant, at CIA headquarters.

"What I have learned regarding Paine so far is not good news," Rafferty continued, pausing from the examination of his notes to glance up at Brock.

"Why am I not surprised?" was the Director's dry, rhetorical reply. His features assumed an even deeper look of displeasure, and he seemed to be bracing himself internally for what he was about to hear. Brock pushed his glasses up on his nose with the tip of one finger, then rocked back in his upholstered swivel chair and laced his fingers behind his head. "Let's get it over with, George. The suspense is killing me."

"I started by calling up everything we have on him in Octopus," Rafferty said. "Personal background, service record, fitness evaluations, and the like. None of it was reassuring. Paine had a pretty grim childhood. It didn't do his attitude any good. By the time he entered adolescence, he had a good head start on becoming a hoodlum. He was a violent rebel even then. He was kicked out of school repeatedly and had numerous minor run-ins with the law. The general opinion seems to have been that he was destined for a life of crime."

"That pretty well describes his function for

the Company," Berghold remarked. The looks he received from both Brock and Rafferty made him wish he'd kept the observation to himself.

"He ended up in Vietnam by being given the choice between military service and his first serious stretch in a penitentiary." Rafferty paused at the quiet groan emitted by the Director.

"For what crime, pray tell? Child molestation, I suppose," Brock said bleakly.

"No. Felonious assault on a police officer. His problems with authority go way back," Rafferty replied.

"Of course. Continue," Brock said.

"The war seems to have been the great turning point of Paine's life. That was when he found his calling, so to speak. He volunteered for every perilous, isolated, and unorthodox type of assignment right from the start. Long-range Reconnaissance Patrols. Tunnel-ratting. The kind of jobs that make commandos nervous. Things that even the best soldiers don't have the stomach for, or the death wish, whatever it takes," Rafferty said.

"He didn't act like a man with a death wish last night," Berghold commented. This time it was his turn to toss a heated look in Rafferty's direction.

"Your point is well made," Rafferty conceded. His eyes lost their focus for a moment as he seemed to consider what it was that drove the man he was describing. "It seems not so much like a wish for death as a fatal attraction with how close he can get to the edge and still survive. It is one of the ways in which he is quite unique."

Rafferty's eyes recovered their focus and returned to the notes he held in his hands. "He soon acquired a reputation for being nerveless, bloodthirsty, and difficult to control. That was what brought him to the attention of the operatives in charge of the Phoenix Program. Spotting men who thrived on wetwork, natural assassins, and recruiting them was part of their job description.

"When they contacted Paine, he had just volunteered for his second tour of duty, and he was working as a headhunter around Khe Sanh." Rafferty paused then, expecting some reaction to this last grim tidbit. Berghold did not disappoint him.

"Shit," the Internal Security chief whispered, closing his eyes and lowering his forehead to the fingers of his left hand, which began to massage it.

"Headhunter?" Brock inquired. "You don't mean...?"

"No, Lucian. He didn't collect them. He was a sniper. A sharpshooter. He put rather large rifle slugs in them. At distances of a thousand yards or better. He had quite a reputation for it at the time. He specialized..." Rafferty stopped for a second, as if reconsidering what he was about to say.

"Go on, George," the Director ordered.

"He specialized in high-ranking officials," Rafferty continued, meeting the Director's eyes. "Men who were supposed to be impossible to get to."

"And now he's back in the neighborhood, and pissed off," Brock said. "That's comforting."

"It gets worse," Rafferty replied.

"Christ," Berghold muttered.

"Paine excelled as a member of Phoenix. If anything, he did his job too well. Became known as something akin to the Wrath of God even among that bunch. Some of his wilder exploits drew political heat when rumors of atrocities surfaced. The real problems between him and the Company only occurred, however, when his personal code of ethics was violated," Rafferty said.

"Personal code?" Brock inquired.

"Yes," Rafferty continued. "It is evidently characteristic of men like Paine to have almost fanatical beliefs regarding matters of honor, justice, loyalty, and the like. They have a highly developed sense of right and wrong. In their own way, they are very moral."

"How romantic," Berghold remarked. He made it sound like "How moronic."

"Exactly," Rafferty replied, "but everyone who has worked with him, both during the war and since, has learned that one either respects his code or pays the penalty for violating it. He is entirely sincere about it."

"A sincere assassin," Brock remarked.

"So it seems," Rafferty continued. "The episode in which his friend Kevin Cunningham was severely wounded is an excellent case in point."

"You have Cunningham under surveillance, I presume?" Brock directed the question at Berghold.

"Yes, sir. We're all over him. At a distance," Berghold responded.

"Cunningham stepped on a mine that was not where it was supposed to be, due to some alleged negligence on the part of the ARVN forces in the area. It did quite a job on him, as we all know from working with him." Rafferty glanced from Brock to Berghold. Both nodded solemnly in response. They knew Cunningham, a specialist in Russian affairs there at Langley, was living proof of how terribly a human being could be damaged and still survive. His motorized wheelchair could be seen cruising the corridors of the vast building daily. Cunningham was still a comparatively young man, but he'd already spent nearly two decades learning how to cope with the loss of both legs and the better part of one arm.

"Most men, even good friends," Rafferty went on, "would have given up on what was left of Cunningham. They were far from the nearest help, in deep jungle, in the heart of *Indian country*, as hostile territory was known at the time. But not Paine. He carried Cunningham out on his back. An incredible act of heroism, really. For which he received the Silver Star."

"He has a number of other decorations, doesn't he?" Brock asked.

"Everything but the CMH itself, yes. And he was nominated for that several times. I imagine it was his knack for aggravating his commanders that kept him from it," Rafferty replied. "Shortly after he got Cunningham out, Paine went AWOL, more or less, disappeared back into the bush...where he proceeded to exact bloody retribution from all those he felt were responsible for Cunningham's injuries. Most of them were friendlies.

"Under the circumstances, it was impossible to make murder charges stick against him. Any witnesses who could have testified against him were either dead or too terrified to cooperate. So he was simply demoted two grades for the unauthorized absence. No one doubts, however, that Paine went on a killing spree to settle up the account for his friend," Rafferty concluded.

"And we still recruited him?" Brock asked, leaning forward to rest his arms on the desk.

"Such men are very valuable assets, Lucian," Rafferty replied. "Volatile and hard to manage, but indispensable when certain jobs have to be done."

"Like nitroglycerine," Brock said.

"Yes," Rafferty agreed with a shrug and a sigh. "He was pursued with the understanding that his usefulness to the Company would be limited, and it has been. He has always worked in sanction and related areas, and he has always been a pain in the ass for whoever runs him. Paine doesn't give a damn about whom he offends. Diplomacy is completely beyond him."

"I wonder why he has continued with us for so long if he so despises authority and supervision, and all that," Brock said.

"There aren't too many places where a man like Paine can get paid for doing what they're best at," Rafferty replied matter-of-factly. "It's us or the Cosa Nostra, and they don't have pension plans, from what I hear." Rafferty returned his attention to the sheaf of papers he held, flipping through them until he found the pages he was seeking.

"All of this is preliminary to what I have to say next. I got Benjamin Hornstein, our chief psychologist, down here at three A.M. for an expert opinion on what we could expect from Paine." Rafferty indulged himself in a pregnant pause, letting the tension mount for a few seconds before he continued. It was apparent that he, at least, was most impressed by what he had been told.

"I expected Hornstein to need at least a couple of hours to come up with a prognosis, but he came to my office as soon as he arrived, and laid it all out for me as if it were very elementary stuff. For him, I suppose, it is," Rafferty said.

"Hornstein said it would be difficult to find a worse sort of person to push. If you come down hard enough on a man like Paine, you could have a world-class nightmare on your hands. He calls him a 'psychic sport,' a one-in-a-million kind of oddity. He reminded me that Paine's *working parts* aren't arranged in a normal configuration. He has some major gears missing from his transmission.

"The good doctor thinks we should keep in mind that one of them is *reverse*. He isn't the type you can scare off. He won't react as one of us would in his situation. A *normal* individual would probably already have gone to pieces if subjected to the pressure he's been under since the operation went sour in East Germany. But Paine isn't normal." Rafferty paused for a moment.

"Hornstein says there's a good chance Paine's

enjoying himself. Personalities like his *thrive* on disaster. Putting heat on them only improves their performance. That's the change that's been taking place. It's the reverse of what you would expect. He's not falling apart. He's coming together; tightening up," Rafferty said.

"Make my day," Berghold muttered.

"What was that?" Brock asked, turning toward him.

"Nothing, sir. Sorry. Just a line from a movie that popped into my mind," Berghold replied.

Brock turned his attention back to Rafferty.

"I get the impression Hornstein thinks the best policy with Paine would be to just leave him alone and hope that he goes away," Brock said.

"That's very close to his opinion, Lucian, yes. He didn't say so outright, but everything he *did* say was to the effect that aggressive action against Paine was a sure loser," Rafferty said.

"Regardless," Brock responded calmly, "case closed."

"I informed the doctor as much," Rafferty replied. "He seemed to find that amusing. He asked me if I knew much about werewolves, believe it or not."

"Werewolves?" Berghold asked incredulously.

"What in God's name do they have to do with this?" Brock asked.

"He said if we go all out to demote Paine, the effect on him could be similar to that of a full moon on a werewolf. We could turn him into a merciless monster. How's that for a colorful image?" Rafferty tried to smile, but succeeded only in grimacing instead.

"Did he advise us to prepare some silver bullets just in case?" Berghold asked Rafferty disgustedly.

"It sounds to me like our chief psychologist moonlights, excuse the expression, as a witch doctor. All we need is some rank superstition to spice things up around here. I want his file on my desk this afternoon, George. Hornstein might be happier returning to private practice," Brock said.

"It's done," Rafferty replied.

"Did Hornstein have anything more enlightened to impart to us? Did he beleaguer you with the hoary analogy between the Company and Dr. Victor Frankenstein, who fell victim to the creature he created?" Brock asked.

"Yes, he did, since you ask. I was going to spare you that," Rafferty answered.

"That was decent of you, George," Brock said.

"Hornstein's closing remarks were that Paine is *not* nuts. He's *worse*. Psychotics are their own undoing eventually since their control and grasp of reality is a sometime thing. Paine is what he calls a 'borderline personality.' The worse his situation gets, the more alert and lethal he becomes. It's nearly impossible to say with any accuracy what he will do, but there are several things Hornstein thinks we can rely on.

"If Paine is still running, he's running *toward*

us, not away. The longer he is loose, the more dangerous he will become. And—" Rafferty hesitated—"it's conceivable *we* are in more jeopardy than Paine is."

3

"You look tired," Paine said. "You should take better care of yourself."

"I've been losing sleep," Cunningham responded, "worrying about a friend."

The two men faced each other from opposing ends of the living room. Paine had been there waiting when he arrived. Cunningham had been shaken to see him standing there, but not really surprised. He had expected Paine to grow weary of evasive maneuvers before too long, and take the offensive, regardless of the odds against him, and the uproar at Langley throughout the day was proof that he had.

Cunningham had known Paine too well and too long to be surprised by such displays of daring. But Paine was now charged with an impressive array of felonies, with murder and treason topping the list. To be seen in his company was to be branded his accomplice. Which spelled an end to Cunningham's career...for starters. An end to all he'd been doing behind the scenes to influence the outcome of his friend's troubles.

That shook Cunningham, knowing as he did that he was under constant surveillance and continuous suspicion of being in league with Paine... as he was. But, he reminded himself, Paine knew all of this, as well. And Paine might risk his own skin, but he would do nothing that would put a friend in peril. That was the kind of man he was. That was the kind of man he had always been.

If John Paine had a fatal flaw, loyalty was probably it.

"Welcome back, John," Cunningham said, "Would you care for a drink?" With his left hand, he pressed the lever that served as both steering wheel and accelerator of his wheelchair. The electric motor whined softly as he rolled across the carpet toward the liquor cabinet.

"Make mine club soda on the rocks with a twist if you've got it. I need to stay as sharp as possible for the next few days," Paine replied.

"I've got it," Cunningham said, "and I couldn't agree more." As he busied himself with the one-handed preparation of the drinks, Paine watched him.

It had been a long time since he had met with his old friend face-to-face. As usual, the sight of Cunningham's blasted body turned a blade deep in Paine's insides. There was always an element of guilt in the anguish he felt toward Cunningham's condition. It was irrational, Paine knew. He wasn't responsible for it. But it was there to haunt him, nonetheless. There was even a name for it. He'd come upon it more than once in his extensive reading about the war. It was called "survival guilt." It arose when someone you cared about bought it while you lucked out.

There was no real clear explanation for it, to Paine's recollection. It was just another one of those glitches to be found in the infinite circuitry of the mind that humans got to contend with when the great organ in the sky decided to take a leak in their direction.

And combat troops weren't the only ones who got stuck with it. Anyone who survived, but lost someone in the process, was fair game. People who walked away from plane crashes were a good example. What was so unique about them that they should go untouched while so many other fine people should perish?

The answer, of course, was that there was no reason. It just happened that way. It could as easily have been you. It simply wasn't ... this time. That sounded reasonable to most people's minds. The problem was, it didn't make sense to their hearts.

Although John Paine was abnormal in some respects, in this he was an average man. He doubted he would ever feel differently about it. Some things were more than you could accept. There had been ample time for him to adjust to it, but it was Cunningham alone who'd come to terms with his misfortune.

Paine admired him for it, knowing that a lesser man would have been ruined by it. He doubted that he could have carried such a terrible burden so well himself.

"They knew I was coming, and I don't know how they knew. I don't like that," Paine said. "It makes me wonder how many other people know things that I think they don't know." He seated himself on the couch, and waited for Cunningham to bring him his drink before motoring back to retrieve his own. Paine had learned long before that his friend resented special treatment on account of his handicap.

"The world is full of eyes, John," Cunningham said as he returned to a position facing Paine from several feet away. "Lately, most of them seem to be turned in your direction. A few of those that aren't have been watching me. Now that they know you're back, I'm sure their number will increase. We must both take care." Cunningham met Paine's gaze, raising his tumbler of bourbon in a toast.

"Don't worry. The people they have on you are asleep at the switch. You're too obvious for the Company to take you too seriously," Paine said, returning the toast.

"You always were way ahead of your opponents, John, and you still are, aren't you?" Cunningham said.

"No. That's a fool's point of view. I'm not way ahead of anyone. If I were, they wouldn't have gotten so close to me more than once. And I'd know who the traitor is inside the Company, wouldn't I? The one who got this ball rolling in the first place, and the one who keeps it rolling, if I'm not mistaken," Paine said.

"Is that why you're here? To take on the mole on his home ground?" Cunningham asked.

"Of course. Working close is the only approach to warfare I understand," Paine said.

Cunningham nodded in response, silent as he worked his tie loose and removed it from around his neck. "You understand if the mole feels threatened by you, it will be easier for him to move against you now. Closeness works both ways."

"I'm betting I'm better at staying alive than he is at making me dead. It's a chance I have to take. He's good at hiding. I'm not. He can outwait me if we play his game. Maybe if I play mine for a while, he'll decide to play it with me," Paine said. He raised his glass to his lips, breathing the scent of the lime that nestled among the ice cubes, and enjoying it.

"Do you think he will?" Cunningham asked.

"I don't know," Paine replied with a shake of his head. "Probably. I'll be doing my best to be a threat. I doubt he'll stand for that for too long. The question is, will he reveal himself when he does whatever he decides to do? That depends on a number of things, including how sly he is and how bad he wants me."

"Will you be staying here in D.C.?" Cunningham asked, taking another hard pull on his drink.

"No. I'll use New York City as my base. I have a small place there on the Upper East Side near the UN. It's handy having an overpopulated third world country an easy commute from here. You can't beat it if you're looking to blend in," Paine responded.

"How will I get in touch with you if I need to?" Cunningham said.

"It'll be safer if I'm the one who does the getting in touch, I think. That way I can keep it to a minimum. We can't afford to be too regular about it. The people who are watching you may be sloppy, but they're not in a coma. We can't expect to get too much past them." Paine underscored the point with a look that said they were playing a deadly game in which there was no room for even a minor indiscretion.

Cunningham finished his drink and backed the chair around on his way to the cabinet for a refill. "You've been calling the plays so far, good buddy, and I haven't objected once, have I?"

"No, but I get the feeling you're about to," Paine spoke to his friend's broad-shouldered retreating silhouette.

"You're right, John." Cunningham raised his voice so Paine could hear him from the other side of the room. "Now that you're back, we should be working as a team like we did back in Nam. We were a dangerous combination then. I think we still are. But we can't be a team unless you include me in what you're doing." As he waited for Paine's reply, Cunningham poured two fingers of Cabin Still into his tumbler.

John Paine didn't answer immediately. It went against his instincts to team up with anyone anymore. Even Kevin Cunningham. The war was ancient history by now. Paine had been operating solo for a long time, and he liked it that way. But it was true that the two of them had been a formidable pair at one time. And by asking for his help, he had drawn Cunningham into deep involvement in a situation that could destroy him. Paine realized he was hardly in a position to keep dictating the way the game would be played. Not to a man who had nearly as much to lose as himself; and the only one upon whom he'd been able to depend from the start.

"I've already asked you for too much, Kevin, and I'm about to ask for more. All I want to do is keep enough distance between us so that you don't go down with me if I fall," Paine explained.

When Cunningham turned and rolled back with the fresh drink in his hand, he was wearing a conspiratorial smile. "Why don't you let me worry about my own ass for a change, okay? I may not be all there physically, but there's nothing wrong with my mind. I can take care of myself."

Paine nodded his agreement. "I'm sure you can. I've never doubted that."

"I think I've earned the right to a full partnership in this thing, and that's what I want. I want to do everything I can to help you clear your name. I owe you my life, John. It's the least I can do. You didn't let the risk stop you when I needed you. I'm not going to let it stop me when you're the one in need," Cunningham said.

"All right, Kevin. You're in. We'll work together on it. Just like old times," Paine said.

"Good. Now we're cooking," Cunningham said. When he noticed the dark cast that had come over Paine's features, he added, "What's wrong?"

"They say every friendship only has so much tread on it. I'm afraid that before this is over, ours will suffer a blowout. I've been putting some hellish miles on it, and I know it," Paine said, looking into Cunningham's eyes.

"No matter what happens, John, it won't change my feelings toward you. That's a promise," Cunningham said.

"That's good enough for me," Paine replied. "Now, on to the next favor."

"Fire away," Cunningham said.

"I have a hunch that the mole is someone close to us, one of the major players in all that's been happening," Paine said.

"Sounds reasonable," Cunningham said, nodding.

"That reduces the number of possibles to a handful. I want to run extensive background checks on all of them. Maybe I can spot something that's been missed until now. Some telltale fact that looks innocent on its face, but maybe not so innocent if the person who's doing the looking is expecting treason. As I will be," Paine said.

"I don't know, John. No one gets into the Company without exhaustive investigation by the Bureau. You know that. Paranoia is what those guys are paid for," Cunningham replied.

"Yes, but their lives don't depend on it. Mine does. That could make all the difference," Paine said.

"Granted. But all that information is locked away in Octopus. You know that," Cunningham said.

"That's where you come in, amigo. I need you to supply me with the daily codes so I can access the computer from an outside terminal," Paine said. There it was. The request was made. He waited to see what Cunningham would do with it.

Cunningham's expression changed appreciably then. He lowered his eyes, staring down into the space where his legs had been once upon a time. Before he donated them, along with one arm, to a hopeless cause.

It was John Paine's turn to ask, "What's wrong?"

"If anyone notices the access, it won't take a genius to figure out who's doing it and how he got the codes," Cunningham said, raising his head to look at his friend again.

"I'll be in and out fast every time, hit and run, before they know there's been an invasion. You know that. What's eating you? You said you wanted in. That means you'll be taking chances," Paine said. He didn't understand Cunningham's reluctance.

"You sure you won't just be wasting your time while you're risking our necks? You're talking twenty to thirty years worth of detailed information to collate on each individual. That's one hell of a lot of effort, even if you're only targeting a few people," Cunningham said. He looked and sounded uneasy with the whole idea.

"Trust me, all right? There hasn't been a mole on record who couldn't have been nailed through their background if someone had taken a close enough look at the facts. Do you have a better idea? If so, I'm all ears. Otherwise, what's the problem?" Paine asked forcefully.

Cunningham's expression changed then, as if he had just arrived at some conclusion. "No problem, John. You're right. I don't know why I was so hung up about it. Maybe the pressure's getting to me."

"Or the bourbon," Paine replied with a slight smile. "I'd go easy on that stuff from now on if I were you. You'll need to be in good form, too, *partner*."

"Good point," Cunningham agreed, setting the remainder of his drink on the coffee table next to the wheelchair.

"I have another suggestion that I think might help our cause in the days ahead," Paine said.

"Which is?" Cunningham inquired.

"From now on, go easy on your defense of me when you're dealing with the Company. In fact, you might even have a change of heart. It could occur to you that your loyalty has been misplaced. What do you think?" Paine asked, sitting forward on the couch, resting his thick forearms on his knees.

"Quit being Paine's one-man cheering section, you mean. Decide to back the *winning side* for a change?" Cunningham said with a smile.

"Exactly. Join the opposition. That should help to reduce the heat on you somewhat. They'll spend less time watching you if you seem to have turned against me. As long as it seems believable. I leave that part up to you," Paine said.

"It sounds like a dirty trick from the master thereof," Cunningham said, brightening visibly. "I should have thought of it myself. That's what too many years pushing paper will do to you. Turn you into a bureaucrat. While I've been perfecting the art of office politics, you've been out there living by your wits, doing the real thing." Cunningham used his muscular left arm to shift his weight in the chair, trying to ease the discomfort with which he lived constantly. "To be frank, there are times when I envy you."

"Don't, Kevin. It's like everything else in life. It looks better from a distance. But once you get close enough, you can see all the warts." Paine pushed himself off the couch, rising slowly to his full height. He twisted his torso from side to side and yawned like a man with jet lag who was several days behind on his sleep. "Believe me, it's more like being John Dillinger than James Bond. Lots of dark alleys and cheap hotels and taking showers with your gun. It gets old. And recently it's been getting older by the hour," Paine concluded, rolling his head around to ease the tension in his neck.

"So what's your battle plan?" Cunningham asked.

"It's real simple. Stay alive and cause trouble. You'll see. And real soon."

When John Paine slipped out into the night and low-crawled across Cunningham's manicured lawn, none of the watchers from the Company observed his progress.

But Martina Vlota did. From her perch on a limb of the old maple behind the house, she missed nothing that Paine did. She had missed nothing since she began the stalk weeks before in Rome. Her hatred for him was a huge black beast inside her, hungry for revenge. And she would have it. She would feed him to the beast. But first she would play with him some more.

Prolong his suffering. As he had prolonged hers.

She might kill the cripple as she had the priest in Vienna, the pathetic old lush who was too drunk to even notice when she slit his throat. Then Paine would lose one more of his rare friends, and all the fools who pursued him would again presume that he had done it himself. It was all so simple, really, and so delicious. Before she was done with him, Paine would have paid in full for what he had done to her, and there would be no doubt as to which of them was the best.

Vlota would erase the humiliating stain of his victory over her on that damned night when she should have died and did not.

She dropped to the ground catlike, soundless, and moved off after him. A graceful, flowing shadow. She would take no chance on losing him again as she nearly had in France after putting a bullet into the thug named Mitchell. She had done so to keep him from taking Paine into custody, and thus ending her little game with him. That Paine had remained at large was reward enough for the risk she took at the time. That he was then charged with Mitchell's murder was merely icing on the cake of her extended retribution.

But then Paine had managed to give Vlota the slip, and had it not been for someone on his side who must hate him as much as she did, he would have been lost to her. But that helpful individual had conveyed Paine's new identity to someone who had, in turn, passed it to Albanian intelligence, her employer. And that was all the help she needed to find him again.

It had given Vlota great pleasure to board the 747 with Paine in London, knowing that he did not know that she was there, watching him and waiting for his next move.

It was essential to her revenge that she stay close to him while remaining invisible. Each day was further proof that no matter how good he was, how skilled and accomplished, she was better. Proof to him. Proof to others like the two of them. Proof to Vlota herself. Then it would be understood that he had beaten her through mischance, and nothing more. Not because she was the blundering, stupid, careless buffoon she had seemed when he had taken her.

Before it was over, no one would dare accuse her of being a typical example of the peasant mentality that abounded in her country in general, and its secret service in particular.

Martina Vlota would bury that misimpression once and for all before she was finished.

Bury it like the smell of death itself beneath the lid of John Paine's coffin.

4

The bullet-proof black stretch Mercedes whispered through the opulent Chevy Chase quiet as if it were loath to rupture the early morning tranquility. In the privacy of his enclosed compartment in the rear, Lucian Brock applied himself fully to the morning edition of the *New York Times*. He knew he could read what interested him in it, the *Washington Post*, the *Wall Street Journal*, and the *National Review* before they reached the guard shack at Langley, but only if he kept his mind focused and gave it his entire attention.

Behind the wheel, his bodyguard/driver, Lou Tobin, was more vigilant than normal. And "normal" for Tobin was similar to "normal" for the Secret Service: hyperalert, with his gun hand never far from the pistol grip of the Ingram M/11–380 he carried in a shoulder holster beneath his sport coat.

Tobin knew that one of the Company's most formidable operatives had turned rogue; was probably in the area; and was killing anyone who dared to take action against him. The man in the back of the limo had issued a termination order on the renegade, John Paine, and it was likely that Paine either knew or assumed that he had. Thus, there was a strong chance that Brock was at the top of the assassin's hit list.

It was Tobin's opinion, and that of numerous other men like him in the Company, that Paine had not been turned by the opposition. He had simply gone psycho. It was far from unheard-of among such professional hatchet men, who were usually no more than marginally sane at best. They were left in the field too long, drifting slowly and imperceptibly, but steadily, closer to the edge until they finally went over.

Then some poor bastard whom they trusted, often the man who recruited them, had to risk getting killed in order to get close enough to "retire" the crazy before he could do any more damage. The sooner it happened to Paine, the better. There was no telling what a man with his skill and experience might do if his mind snapped: go after all the top men in the intelligence community; try for the President himself; start killing everyone who had ever bugged him, in alphabetical order.

When the traffic cop on the motorcycle appeared in his rearview mirror, mounted on the door beside him, Tobin noted his presence, then discounted him. All the local law knew better than to treat any of the government power brokers who lived in the D.C. equivalent of Beverly Hills like average citizens. It was, therefore, a surprise to Tobin when the cop closed the distance between them and put on his flashers as they were passing through a stretch of woodlands.

When Tobin ignored him, the cop accelerated up beside him. "Pull over!" he barked, jabbing the black-gloved index finger of his right hand toward the side of the road. Then the big Honda scooted in front of the Mercedes, slowed, and then braked to a stop. The big man kicked the stand down, dismounted from the motorcycle, and removed the book of citations from the bracket where it rested next to the radio.

"Badge-heavy moron," Tobin muttered as the officer strode back to stand next to his window. The driver checked his watch reflexively. If they were late arriving at Langley, Brock, who was lost in his newspapers behind the blackened windows in back, would have his ass on toast.

"May I see your license and registration, sir?" the cop said. Tobin could not tell if the man was looking at him due to the mirror shades he wore beneath his white helmet.

Probably wears them when he works nights, too, Tobin thought. *A regular storm trooper. Figures they'll get him laid if he points them at enough secretaries on the way to work.*

"My license and registration? You must be kidding!" Tobin made no move to do anything, simply examining the cop through the window with contemptuous disbelief.

"Do I look like I'm kidding, son?" The cop flipped open the book of tickets and removed the pen clipped to it as he spoke.

"No. You look like a guy who's growing old working traffic because he's too dumb for his own good," Tobin replied with a sneer.

The exposed portion of the cop's face betrayed a patience that was rapidly eroding under the driver's abuse.

"Why don't you step out of the car, boy, where I can take a look at you?" the cop said, lowering the book slightly and taking a step back away from the door.

Tobin checked his watch again and fumed. This wasn't supposed to happen. It was so unlikely, he'd never been told how to handle it should it occur.

"Don't you care about your job? Is that it? You looking for early retirement... like this afternoon? Do you know who's back there?" Tobin gestured to the rear with a jerk of his head.

"I don't care if Jesus and his disciples are back there passing the wine. I'm telling you nicely to hit the pavement. One last time." The cop's voice had gone flat and threatening.

Snarling obscenities, Tobin opened the door and stepped out of the car as the cop glanced in both directions to check for traffic.

That was when Lou Tobin glanced at the cop's feet and saw the penny loafers he was wearing.

Being the professional that he was, Tobin wasted no time cursing himself for his carelessness. He simply went for the Ingram with all of his considerable speed. He had it in his hand, and was bringing the muzzle to bear on the impostor when the man kicked it from his grip.

Tobin let the weapon go. He was more than capable of killing without it. He launched a side kick at the cop's chest. Tobin was young and tough, a third-degree black belt in Tae Kwon

Do, and it showed. The kick was pinpoint lightning, delivered with crippling force. However, his opponent, who appeared old enough to be his father, was as fast as Tobin himself. He twisted out of the way; blocked the foot with his forearm; and drove a spin kick of his own into Tobin's crotch. His attacker's foot caught Tobin just above its tender intended targets, hurting him as it drove him back against the doorframe, but doing little to disable him.

For seconds they sparred, feeling each other out, searching for an opening. They did it wordlessly. With the charade over, the two men now understood each other well. They were brethren. One of them was about to die. That was the only way it could turn out once combat was joined.

If there was an obvious advantage, it belonged to the impostor. The reflective glasses made it impossible for Tobin to watch his eyes.

They parried, feinted, deflected one another's kicks and punches. It was all very fast and savage and eerily quiet. Then Tobin fired a knife hand at the other man's throat, lost his balance for an instant, and sensed the elbow rifling toward his temple the instant before bone smashed into nerve and bone. The blow probably killed Tobin as it had a number of other men, but the cop was taking no chances. Not with the likes of Lou Tobin. He demonstrated his respect by following the elbow with a right-handed heel strike to the youth's chin that drove his head back, exposing the large kill zone beneath it.

Then... the two-knuckled death blow had

taken years to learn. Like so many other techniques that the uninitiated were sure could be mastered in one, or possibly two, intensive weekends. He had practiced it so many times, driving the hand with all his upper body's great strength into padded concrete, that the two joints were fused. He had been forced to learn to write with his left hand as a result. When it was damp and cold, the bones of his right hand hurt all the time.

Tobin's larynx imploded a fraction of a second before his neck broke from the blow.

When the door across from him opened, Lucian Brock reached for his briefcase. He had turned with the valise grasped in one hand, and was sliding across the polished leather seat, when a familiar face appeared in the opening.

Brock froze then, unprepared for that particular face and uncertain as to how to react.

"Good morning, John. You have a way of turning up in the strangest places. We've been looking all over for you," Brock said.

"Good morning, sir. You're not carrying anything, are you?" Paine had removed the helmet and glasses. They went into the woods beside the road with the motorcycle and the mortal shell of Lou Tobin.

"No, John. Wetwork is your specialty, not mine," Brock replied remotely. "I suppose I can assume we're not at Langley." Brock craned his neck to take a look around Paine's leather-clad bulk.

"That's correct, sir. The structure you see behind me is an abandoned barn. I pulled into it to ensure we would not be interrupted. Your vehicle is rather conspicuous," Paine said.

"I see," Brock said. And he did. No interruptions. No hope of rescue. Just the two of them.

Paine couldn't help but admire Brock's grace under pressure. They'd only met once before, and then formally, but Paine had taken advantage of the opportunity to form certain impressions. One of them had just been validated. Whatever else the Director of the Central Intelligence Agency might be, the man was no coward.

"So now you've added kidnapping to your inventory of transgressions," Brock said, setting the briefcase aside and returning to a more comfortable position on the seat.

"That's right," Paine replied.

"And Lou? Did he survive this latest demonstration of your gall?" Brock inquired, crossing his legs casually at the knee and leaning back into the upholstery.

"I'm afraid not, sir," Paine responded.

The patrician's lips formed a brief moue of distaste. He lowered his eyes to his hands, studied them for a moment, then sighed. "I'll miss him. He was a good man."

"Yes. He was," Paine said.

"But not good enough, obviously," Brock added.

"He was young and inexperienced," Paine said.

"But that doesn't describe either you or I, does it, John?" Brock inquired, meeting his captor's eyes directly.

"No, sir. It doesn't," Paine answered.

"And what of the policeman from whom you *borrowed* that uniform? Did you kill him, too?" Brock asked.

"No. He was easy. He'll be fine in a few days. I would have spared your driver if I could. I tried. But he figured it out before I could get to him. Then I had no choice," Paine said.

"No. I don't suppose you did," Brock replied. "Why don't you come in and sit down, John? That is, unless you have something less civilized than conversation in mind for this little encounter." Brock's last words were delivered calmly and without inflection. He knew full well that Paine might have bloody plans for him, plans that Brock's resistance could do no more than postpone for a few desperate moments. If that was the case, the scion of two centuries of wealth and privilege intended to comport himself with dignity and courage to the bitter end.

"You can relax, Mr. Brock. I'm not here to harm you. Enough harm's been done already," Paine said as he stepped into the compartment and seated himself on the opposite end of the bench, facing his boss. "I've come to tell you there is a traitor in the Company, and it's not me."

"You've hardly been acting like a loyal member of the organization of late, have you?" Brock said, studying Paine coolly.

"What would you suggest? That I turn myself in meekly, and wait for the mole to arrange a case of the measles for me before I can cause him any more trouble?" Paine asked.

"Catching the measles" was a euphemism in the game for terminations that were made to appear like death from natural causes. It was the standard method for dealing with operatives who had become an embarrassment, and was much preferred to arrest, prosecution, and all the painful publicity that attended them.

"You're acting rather paranoid, don't you think?" Brock asked with a lift of his brows.

"That's pretty rich under the circumstances, especially coming from you. Let's not snow each other, okay? It's too late for that. This is our last chance to end this thing before more innocent people die. I know you've put a sanction order out on me," Paine said, not really knowing until the look on Brock's silent face confirmed it. "You've done it because you're afraid what I'll do. Despite the fact that I've never given you reason to doubt either my sanity or my loyalty. If that's not paranoia, what would you call it?"

Brock thought that over for a minute. "Once these situations get out of hand, they seem to take on a life of their own. That's true, I'll admit. All of us are programmed to believe the worst, including me," Brock said.

"It's what keeps us alive," Paine responded, "The mole understands all this, and he's taking full advantage of it to turn the Company inside out, getting as many people killed as possible in the process, with my name sitting on top of the list."

"What leads you to believe we have a mole among us?" Brock asked.

"Someone got to Wilson, and convinced him that I was a double. All the evidence supports Wilson's loyalty. Which means when the mission soured, he was prepared to believe I was responsible and would attempt to neutralize him if he didn't take me out first. That's why he tried to kill me. That's also why he took his life after I disabled him. He assumed he had only interrogation and a neck shot to look forward to since he had fallen into enemy hands. If Wilson was loyal, he could only have been disinformed by someone on the inside," Paine concluded.

Brock stared off into space, stroking his neat beard thoughtfully with one hand as he listened closely, taking the entire explanation in. "What about Father Beck and Bill Mitchell? Do you expect anyone to believe a *mole* is responsible for their deaths, as well? I hardly think the traitor would be following you wherever you go, do you?"

"No. I don't. There's someone else. They may be working in cooperation with the mole, but I don't think so," Paine said. Then he noted the look of skepticism that stole over Brock's features. "I know. Conspirators behind every bush. It sounds delusional even to me, but the truth is, I've made a lot of enemies over the years. It's hardly unlikely that one of them might choose coincidentally to pursue a vendetta against me at this time. Father Beck's murder especially bears every indication of someone who kills for sport. He died merely for the sin of being close to me. That's not the way the mole works. He's more subtle than that," Paine said.

"Direct action and indirect being taken against you simultaneously?" Brock speculated.

"So it seems," Paine replied.

"A very potent piece of bad luck for you," Brock continued.

"Yes. I've noticed," Paine said.

"And Mitchell?" Brock inquired. "Why would your nemesis kill a man who was so obviously eager to do that very thing himself?"

Paine looked away for a moment as he considered, the lines in his face deepening as he thought about the one who must bear such a great hatred for him. "There are a number of reasons I can imagine. This is something very personal for whoever it is. I think that pride is involved as well as vengeance. He wants me all to himself. He wants it to go on until he's tired of it. Mitchell got in the way, and was about to take me out of play, so Mitchell died," Paine said.

"This is an awful lump to swallow, John. Viewing you as a kill-crazy renegade makes everything ever so much simpler," Brock said.

"Yes. Everyone loves simple explanations to complex problems. The trouble is, it doesn't wash. If I was a double, I would have been a fool to come home after everything went to hell in East Germany. Father Beck was an old friend of mine. I had nothing to gain by killing him, and any idiot would have realized that I would be the first person to come under suspicion," Paine said, opening his rough hands with the palms toward Brock, as if to say, How could anything be more self-evident?

"I didn't have to kill Mitchell. Mitchell was arrogant incompetence personified. I would have let him live just as a point of professional pride. It would have been sufficient to turn his gun into a suppository. And, again, I was certain to be everyone's chief suspect if he died," Paine said. "None of it floats unless you start with the conclusion that I'm a traitor, and reason your way backward from there."

"Which still leaves the question of whether you haven't simply gone 'round the bend," Brock remarked.

"Would you say that to someone who had?" Paine met his eyes as he said it.

"Probably not," Brock conceded.

"For what it's worth, you're going to walk away from our talk this morning alive and unmolested. That's part of the reason we're having it. I've got you. I can do with you as I please. And I'm letting you go, as a token of my continuing loyalty, a sign of good faith, and proof that I'm not a drooling maniac," Paine said.

"I appreciate that," Brock responded sincerely. "And I am duly impressed... just as you intended. I assure you I will take immediate action to bring this incestuous bloodshed to an end. You have my word on it." Brock nearly extended his hand, then thought better of it. He was already closer to his executioner than he ever cared to be.

"That would be wise of you, sir. I am tired of having your hounds behind me. If you don't want me to act like an animal... don't treat me like one. If you chase anything long enough, you will bring it to bay. Then it will turn on its pursuers and show them its rage. I'm losing patience with attempts on my life." Paine rose from the seat and backed toward the open door. "Believe me, Mr. Brock, you don't want to see my rage. Some quarry are better lost than caught. Especially large predators. Think it over."

Then John Paine was gone, leaving Lucian Brock alone with his perspiration in the back of his shiny black Mercedes.

You don't want to see my rage. Paine's words echoed in the Director's mind.

"I don't think you'll find mine all that attractive either, Mr. Paine," Brock said to the silence as he reached for his phone.

"He could have butchered me for his sick amusement if he'd cared to!" Brock's words were poisoned darts hurled across his desk at his subordinate.

Mark Berghold stood at rigid attention. He had never seen the man so incensed, and prayed to whoever might be listening that he would never see him that way again.

"He could have skinned me alive!" Brock stretched the last syllable, leaning toward Berghold as if tempted to do something similar to the man responsible for his personal safety.

"Lou Tobin..." Berghold was about to say that Tobin was as good as any of the hired guns who watched over the President. It might not be much of a defense, but it was the truth. Only a handful of people in the world could have gotten past him. Unfortunately, Paine was numbered in that handful.

"Tobin was the best you have! I don't need to be told that! And Tobin was light work for him! This isn't some half-assed Palestinian you're dealing with. Not Black September or the Red

Brigade. This is a man who's been killing those barbarians for years and making it back alive for debriefing," Brock said. His eyes never left Berghold's face.

"I want him *dead*! I want him run to ground. Use every available means at your disposal," Brock said.

"Carte blanche, sir?" Berghold asked, wanting to get it on the record.

"What does it sound like to you, Berghold?" Brock inquired with heavy sarcasm.

"It sounds like carte blanche, sir," Berghold replied.

"I want every cop in the country to make John Paine his top priority. There will be no safe place for him. He thinks he is above the law; that he can return to this country and do as he pleases. We'll see about that," Brock said.

"But you still want it done with a minimum of publicity," Berghold said. "Not an open manhunt."

"Of course," Brock answered acidly. "The man is a walking repository of state secrets. There's no calculating the damage he could do if he talked to the wrong people. He's to be neutralized as soon as possible after he's taken into custody."

"And you would prefer that custody be avoided," Berghold said, seeking the clearest picture he could get of the Director's wishes.

"I would prefer that he self-destruct even as we speak," Brock replied.

"Very well, sir," Berghold responded with a nod. "Will that be all, sir?" He was afraid that it wasn't, and his fear was justified.

"Not quite. Tell me, Mark, are you familiar with Afghanistan?" Brock cocked his head to one side, as if he were shifting his line of vision in order to get a better image of Berghold in his sights.

"Not very, sir," And don't know anyone who ever wanted to be, either, he thought. "I've talked with some of our agents who've worked there."

"And what did they think of it, Mark?" Brock asked with feigned bonhomie.

"May I be blunt?" Berghold asked.

"By all means."

"They said if God farted, you'd smell it first in Afghanistan."

"Neither a pleasant place nor a pleasant people?" Brock asked with more false warmth.

"Worse than Utah," Berghold answered with a sober nod.

"If Paine isn't bagged and stuffed for display to any who might be tempted to emulate him, that is where you will be posted, and that is where you will remain until you forget what grass looks like. Would you care for me to repeat that?" Brock said with a smile like an incision.

"No, sir."

"I want his head on a pike by the front gate! I want it done this week! I don't care how you do it! It's that, or you are, by Christ, on your way to Kabul!"

Brock dismissed him with a fierce jerk of his head.

And Mark Berghold was more than happy to go.

5

In the dream, he ran. It was always the same. Something was close behind him. Something swift and starved that needed only one misstep, one wrong move on his part, to close the final feet between them. Then it would launch itself through the air to land with all its massive weight on his back. With jaws agape and claws fully extended. To bring him smashing down to the earth. Never to rise again. Once it had him, it would take its time. Savoring the final moments of its prize. Before it began to feed.

His pursuer was always the same, but the terrain through which they ran would vary from dream to dream. Sometimes it was the jungle, where trip wires and deadfalls littered the path he must follow. Sometimes it was the side streets of Montmartre or Soho, where men with knives sliced at him from each pool of darkness he plunged through. Always there was death both ahead and behind. Always he must run with all his strength, regardless of how tired he might be.

Paine twisted in his sleep, breathing hard, his breath hissing between clenched teeth. Then, suddenly, he was awake, with his heart hammering in his chest, bathed in sweat, and knowing something was wrong.

First, he commanded his body to be still, taking air in through his nose, then blowing it out evenly through his mouth. He pushed the dream away consciously, as he had many times before, sending it back to his depths, where it belonged. When it was gone, he formed an image of his lurching heart in his mind's eye and willed it to slow its pace.

Paine listened. He probed the bedroom of the flat, making sure he was alone before he opened his eyes. Then he extended the radius of his search to the rest of the apartment. He listened. He turned his hearing up as high as it would go. For five minutes he waited for some tiny, telltale sound. When none occurred, he spread the web of his senses a step further. To the fifth floor hallway...

where he heard movement. Not the honest footfalls and clattering locks of the building's other tenants returning home from some lengthy indiscretion in the middle of the night, or the morning, depending on one's opinion of 3:00 A.M.

This was the stealthy signature of people trying to make no sound at all. The creak of a concealed floorboard beneath a heavy body's shifting weight; the rustle of clothing; the distant susurration of covert voices in whispered conspiracies. Paine had heard such sounds enough times before to know what they portended.

He slipped soundlessly off the bed in the T-shirt and jeans in which he'd slept, knowing that somehow they had found him again despite all his precautions. As he worked his feet into his sneakers, he realized that the typical street sounds outside the building were also missing. No passing cars. No voice or tread of any of Manhattan's ubiquitous pedestrians. No audible tokens of life in the vicinity at all.

Paine could picture the way it was. The street running east to west in front of his building, blocked off at both ends. All the building's exits covered. The NYPD manning the perimeter. The FBI in full combat gear strategically distributed from floor to floor. No one taking any chances. All the weapons of the men inside silencer-equipped.

How had they found him? Paine had leased the apartment under an assumed name three years before. It was no more than a barely furnished pied-à-terre that he used only infrequently. It was six months since the last time he had been there. Could he have been tailed to his hideaway despite his elaborate efforts to "dry-clean" his trail? Had a passing cop identified him regardless of his constantly disguised appearance?

Paine could only pose the questions to himself, leaving their further consideration until later, because he knew they would be coming through the door for him at any moment. That was the way it was done. At the darkest hour.

When you had the best chance of catching your opponent at a disadvantage.

He had done it himself that way a score of times. Getting into position, then waiting as the night grew deeper with each passing hour until whoever it was you were after was either lost in sleep or rendered conveniently sluggish by the ebb of his inner rhythms. Only the year before, Paine had terminated one of Manuel Noriega's henchmen in that fashion. Like the thuggish dictator himself, the man lived only for money and power. Also like Noriega, he acquired money by assisting cocaine on its way from Medellín to Orange County, and power, primarily, by murdering all who opposed him. The individual in question, Ferdinand Escobar, was not above drawing out the death agonies of someone who had really gotten under his skin. On occasion, these objects of his bestiality had been norteamericanos.

After someone in Washington tired of this behavior, Paine dropped in on Escobar one Sunday morning at his hacienda on the outskirts of Panama City. It was a solo mission, and Paine had already retired three of Escobar's guards without causing a stir by the time he reached the gangster's bedroom in the perfect stillness of the final moments before the quickening of another tropical sunrise. Paine had timed his visit on the assumption that Escobar was the kind of man who slept lightly, guards or no guards, and in that, Escobar had proven him correct.

Paine had been attempting to line up a shot around the young woman with whom Escobar was entwined in the midst of the vast expanse of the canopied bed when the man awoke. Being the ruthless survivor that he was, Escobar pulled the woman between them and used her as a shield as he lunged toward the nine-millimeter Walther on the bedside table. Thus deprived of a viable option, Paine had been forced to kill them both. Even then, Escobar had the hefty automatic in his grasp when he died.

Some men were best approached at an evil hour.

Even then it might be a problematic proposition.

As it now was for the patriotic men and women of the Bureau who were under orders to apprehend John Paine.

Orders that must have originated in the office of Lucian Brock, Paine realized. It was as clear a statement as he needed of how the Director intended to respond to Paine's declaration of his innocence and the warning he attached to it. This was the way Brock wanted it. To hell with who or how many got hurt. Regardless of where the true guilt might ultimately reside.

Paine didn't want it that way. He'd done all he could, short of getting himself killed, to avoid it. But now the die was cast, and he would do whatever was required to survive. Just as he'd been doing for as long as he could remember.

Paine had selected the flat with the possibility of enemy action as one of his prime considerations. He had plotted avenues of escape, potential diversions he could employ to confuse his assailants and buy himself a few precious minutes of time. Though there was no food in the flat, there was a smorgasbord of explosive hors d'oeuvres, reserved exclusively for unexpected company and special occasions.

None of the tidbits Paine had prepared were lethal. Though killing had always been essential to his vocation, he had never lost his respect for life; had not degenerated into the reflexive butchery of which he'd been accused. Whatever the average peaceful citizen might think of a man like him, Paine considered himself a soldier. Though it was a species of guerrilla war he'd been fighting against his country's enemies since he'd been recruited by the Company, that didn't mean all the classic rules had been suspended. You couldn't redefine right and wrong from day to day as you went along. To act as if you could, was to forsake what was left of your decency.

No. Certain things were understood. They never changed. You only killed the enemy. You did it because they clearly needed killing, and it was your job. There was no pleasure in it, although there might be satisfaction. If there *was* pleasure in it, your clutch was slipping; you'd been in the business too long; it was time for you to get out of it. You never killed your own people. Even if you were under friendly fire, this prohibition applied. The only possible exception came when it was a plain choice between your life and theirs. Even then, it had to be understood as the absolute last resort.

That was the way it had been with Lou Tobin. Paine had known that Brock was the only man who could stop the madness if he chose to do so. He had known, too, that only drastic action would enable him to meet with Brock to state his case and then walk away with his life and his freedom intact. It had been an inescapable question of John Paine's survival in all respects. Still, Paine had risked his life in the attempt to keep from killing Tobin. He could have wasted the bodyguard as soon as he got within range. It would have been the safest thing to do. But Tobin was merely doing his job, and he was not the enemy. So Paine had drawn him out of the car, playing the charade as far as it would go, hoping for the small opening he needed to put the driver out of action temporarily. But then Tobin had made him, because the cop had chanced to be a man with small feet. The instant a gifted killer like Tobin went into action, Paine was forced to fight for his life without restraint. It was bad, but it was unavoidable.

Similarly, one did all one could to avoid harming noncombatants. This was especially difficult, given the nature of the war they were fighting. Battles often took place in the midst of a civilian setting. Nonetheless, it was a soldier's responsibility to risk his life if necessary to spare any neutrals in the vicinity. To do otherwise was to become a terrorist. Terrorists, men and women who thought nothing of slaughtering scores of civilians on the off chance of thereby snuffing some of the opposition, were beneath the contempt of men like Paine. He was sure an especially unpleasant corner of hell was reserved for IRA bombers and their ilk.

But if all one's scruples came to naught, and innocents died anyway, it was incumbent on a soldier to know that he had sinned, and, consequently, to feel guilty and rotten about it.

When that stopped happening, and the heart cared for nothing but its next beat...one had been doing it too long. It was time to find a new line of work before you turned into one of those you had despised for so long.

Therefore, Paine had not rigged the flat with claymores and bouncing Bettys and double-barreled shotguns positioned to neuter the first person to arrive without an invitation. He could have. He knew how. He had the ordnance at his disposal. He had made such terminal arrangements many times before.

But only when he was dead certain who would be killed, and equally certain that they should be. That called for a highly controlled situation. Not an apartment in one of the world's most populated and unpredictable cities. He had no interest in living with the death of the Puerto Rican building superintendent on his conscience. Or, for that matter, of some earnest guy with a badge, a wife, and four loving little ones who depended on him, either.

Paine slipped into the shoulder rig he'd taken from Tobin and checked to be sure the Ingram was firmly seated behind the Velcro fastener in the holster. He jammed the Smith .357 that had once belonged to a motorcycle cop into his waistband. From beneath the bed, he hauled the large canvas tote bag he had stocked for just such a contingency. He hefted it to reassure himself that its contents had remained undisturbed during his prolonged absence.

Paine knew he had to act immediately if he was to take the initiative and sow havoc among his opponents, forcing them unexpectedly into the defensive response he required.

Padding silently from room to room, he activated all the booby traps that were already in place.

Paine had selected a flat with windows that faced on the air well that separated his building from its neighbor to the west, and on the narrow alley in the rear. The fire escape ran up the center of the structure's back wall. Thus, there was no convenient access to his windows. There was only one easy way in... the door that opened on the hall. That was where the invasion would come from.

But they would be watching the windows, as well. No doubt watching them quite closely. Through Starlight scopes mounted on the receivers of high-velocity sniper rifles, more than likely. Like the dogged pursuers of Bonnie Parker and Clyde Barrow, the mob that was after Paine might be slow on the uptake, but they learned from their mistakes. He expected each attempt on him to be more thoughtfully executed than the one that went before. He relied on this assumption because it had saved his bacon repeatedly over the years. Which was more than could be said for Bonnie and Clyde. As a student of the desperado kind, Paine knew the pair had eventually succumbed to their own contempt for their enemies.

That was a terminal stupidity he never intended to commit.

With ten minutes having elapsed since he awoke to the sound of inappropriate murmurs in the hall, Paine could feel the climax of the situation approaching. He knew at any moment they would go to work on the door. With the six deadbolts and the crossbar he had installed, that would keep them busy for a while. There was also no telling how many other angles of approach they might be attempting. Regardless of how badly they wanted him, however, he was sure they would do their best to keep the gunplay to a minimum. They were all individuals like himself. They lived in horror of butchered bystanders.

That meant they wouldn't stand back and pour a few thousand high-caliber rounds into the flat to soften him up for starters, a tactic sometimes referred to as the "Iwo Jima approach." Since Paine was massively outgunned, he found that certainty reassuring. It placed them at a severe disadvantage, despite the odds, and opened up all manner of interesting possibilities.

Paine knew if he were in charge of the operation being mounted against him, one of his first steps would be to cut his flat's phone line at the circuit board in the basement. It might not be necessary, but why take chances? The more isolated a target was, the less likely it was that he'd be causing you problems.

However, when he lifted the receiver to his ear, the dial tone informed him that his pursuers considered that particular precaution unnecessary.

Paine punched out the code for emergency service.

When the operator came on the line, he began to gasp and wheeze as he told her in a frantic whisper that he was trapped by an inferno in his apartment. It was raging out of control; the entire building was going up in flames; people were leaping from tenth-floor windows; there were repeated explosions that shook the building at its base, where a dry cleaning establishment was located.

He begged her for help, cursing the smoke that had driven him to the floor in search of the last inches of breathable air. The woman had to wring the address out of him, as the fumes and the panic overwhelmed him.

Once he was sure she had the address, he broke the connection. Not a brilliant maneuver, and John Paine would be the first to admit it. But if it worked, that was enough for a committed pragmatist. What he needed was a mob, and all the clamor and disorder that went with it. So he had summoned one. His description of the fire had consisted of a worst-case scenario: a flash-blaze feeding on exploding chemicals with a building full of sleeping tenants trapped above the voracious flames. That should be good for three fire companies at the least. Firefighters, like field operatives, stayed alive by presuming the worst and equipping themselves for it in advance. As they raced to the rescue, they would communicate over the emergency channel on their radios. That channel was continuously monitored by every news crew in Manhattan that was on duty. The instant they heard the call, they, too, would be speeding to the scene of such a juicy calamity. Paine estimated fifteen to twenty vehicles were homing in on his distress call at that very moment.

Of course, once they arrived, they would turn immediately around and go home if there was no fire.

But fire was no great challenge.

Not for a man as resourceful as John Paine.

Paine recognized that setting his home on fire was not exactly a moderate solution to his problem, but in all fairness, it was hardly what anyone would call a moderate problem.

Paine removed several white phosphorous grenades from his bag of tricks.

He paused for a moment, holding them in both hands, somewhat reluctant to trigger the pandemonium that the next few hours would be. He savored the silent darkness surrounding him.

Then he pulled the first pin, and lobbed the incendiary through the open bedroom window, out into the night.

5...4...3...2...1...*Krump!*

He heard the charge detonate forty feet below on the roof of the florist shop that separated his building from the next. Suddenly the chasm between the high, sheer walls was filled with a brilliant, cruel, and unnatural light. There were angry shouts from both the street and the alley to assure him that the building was surrounded as he had assumed.

As he pulled the second pin, Paine could picture the evil being wrought by the demon he had released to caper and devour all it touched outside: the churning billows of snowy smoke, the score of hissing and unquenchable conflagrations ignited by the eruption of as many blinding blue-white bits.

Paine had just tossed a grenade into his living room, and was stepping back out of the way, when something hit his front door with terrific, splintering force.

He assumed they were using a steel ram large enough to accommodate the hands and strength of several men. Paine was sure the assault came hard on the explosion of the grenade outside because someone with a radio in the street had informed the men in the hallway that the balloon was going up on some schedule other than their own.

Again the ram smashed into the door. The floor beneath Paine's feet quivered from the blow. Plumes of chemical and wood smoke began to snake along the ceiling from the living room, slithering eagerly into each of the adjoining rooms. A dozen small fires were busy eating everything in range, and expanding as they did, reaching out to one another, anxious to join hands and find strength in unity.

Paine yanked the pins from two more WPs; huddled next to the bedroom window, out of the line of fire; then rifled both through the opening, one to his left toward the street, the other toward the alley.

He smiled. That'll give them something besides me to think about. The detonation of each grenade was followed shortly by barks of fear and warnings, vocal gunshots, from the officers and agents in the vicinity. Paine knew there were few things as effective as flying white phosphorus for getting and keeping an individual's attention.

Again the steel beam careened into the door.

Paine could hear the wood of the door cracking and snapping into kindling beneath the metal fist.

He dipped into the bag again, and as he identified what he sought by feel, he heard sirens approaching in the distance. Right on time, he thought, withdrawing first one and then another tear gas canister from the bag. Pulling the pins of both, he tossed them through the window to contribute to the tumult that was already under way. Paine was willing to bet none of the opposition came prepared to deal with CN gas. That was a real shame. Without masks like the one he had in the bag, breathing and seeing would become a serious hassle for everyone who was exposed. No lasting harm, but for an hour or so it was true misery, and highly disorienting.

He followed the tear gas with several stun grenades. They detonated with a sound and flash equivalent to a bolt of lightning. The thunder from each resonated from one hard surface to the next for blocks all around. It was certain they could be heard by the rapidly nearing fire units. Smoke from the growing blazes already cloaked the building in a roiling mantle of gray-white fog.

I'd like to hear what the fire folks have to say when the Bureau person in charge tells them to stay out of it. If Paine wasn't mistaken, under the circumstances that now applied, in a dispute between the FBI and the NYFD, it was the latter that held undisputed jurisdiction. The ranking fire captain would have every right to tell the nearest NYPD uniform to take any agent who made a fuss into custody, and keep him there until the fire was under control.

Paine found that vision so enchanting that it was nearly worth hanging around just to take it in from the sidelines.

He would have chuckled if it hadn't required all his concentration to identify the smoke grenades in the dark and get them through the window to add some more spice to the devil's brew he was concocting. Some were green. Some red. Some yellow. All resembled the fumes emitted by hazardous substances like naphtha, a solvent used in dry cleaning, fumes that were invariably lethal if inhaled.

Any experienced firefighter's first reaction at the sight of such apparent toxic fumes would be to clear everyone from the area. Absolutely everyone.

The howls and whoops of the sirens rose to a jarring crescendo when the fire trucks arrived. Even from his limited vantage point, Paine sensed the rhythmic pulses of their dazzling lights. The warmth of the summer night blossomed with the amplified static and harsh metallic voices from their radios.

Paine listened to the shouts from the street with grim satisfaction as he pitched one grenade after another through every window he could reach, no longer concerned about the function of each, desiring only to aggravate the chaos into which he was about to flee.

The ram burst through the door, but still its frame held. Guttural curses poured through the opening from the agents in the hall who found themselves forced to tear the door apart in order to enter the flat. Some of the voices sounded desperate to Paine. And well they might. His attackers knew they were no longer in control of the situation, and control was essential to their mission's success. The unmistakable sounds from without assured them the whole thing was falling apart, further deteriorating with each minute that passed.

A flying piece of wood triggered the booby trap nearest the flat's threshold. A stun grenade detonated like the crack of doom, driving the men with the ram away from the door reflexively. The ones closest to the explosion were blinded by the flash. All were temporarily deafened by the boom.

The apartment was filling with smoke, acrid, superheated, suffocating. Paine donned the gas mask seconds before the tear gas canisters set as traps in the living room exploded from the heat, rapidly flooding the flat with caustic vapors carried on the currents of air being driven by the flames.

From the hallway Paine heard new voices, the voices of his neighbors awakened by the clamor; they resonated with anger and fear. They didn't know the fire was still young and easily contained by the firefighters who were even then forcing their way through the police cordon to get to the building and do their job. They only knew all hell itself had broken loose, and they were demanding to know what the menacing thugs outside Paine's apartment had to say about their right to be tearing the place apart.

With the door breached and the CN spreading, the predictable hacking and wails of distress mingled with the belligerent bellows of all concerned.

Paine anchored the rope ladder to the sill of the kitchen window, then pushed the coiled bail of its length through the opening to plummet down the wall. With an agility that belied his size and weight, he hopped into the sink and eased first one leg, and then the other, out over the sheer fifty-foot drop.

Before he started his descent, Paine ignited the fuse of the last item he had extracted from his trick bag, a braided chain of one hundred M–80 firecrackers. It was impossible for him to know what sort of reception might be awaiting him in the strobe-lit, churning canyon of smoke the alley had become. There was a good chance he'd already created enough distractions to enable him to creep through the holes in the net around him undetected.

Nonetheless, he hurled the long string of charges over his shoulder into the rolling gray cloud beneath him.

The rapid fire of reports commenced before the firecrackers reached the alley floor. If Paine hadn't known better, he would have wagered someone had just opened up with a major automatic, like a .45-caliber MAC–10. It was the sort of soul-stirring racket that sent every mother-loving son in search of the nearest cover. That would be the last break he would need to make it safely to the ground, and away from the area undetected.

Paine could not know that the two FBI agents who crouched at the base of the wall directly beneath the quivering bottom rung of the ladder were not deceived. They were men much like Paine himself: smart, canny, fearless, and duty-bound to accomplish their mission. With guns drawn, they prepared to do whatever was required to bag him when he reached the end of his rope.

But Martina Vlota knew they were there. With her slender body pressed flush against the alley's opposite wall, she had watched them for some time. It was mad for her to be there in the midst of the FBI, the police, the firefighters, and God knew who else. The part of her that was still sane understood that, but the part that lived only to avenge itself on Paine was indifferent to the risk. It would not allow his fate to be decided by any hands other than her own.

After all, what was his crime against them compared to the horror he had inflicted upon her? The endless, infinite hours of her solitary struggle to stay alive. The terrible assurance that she could do no more than delay her final, inevitable descent into a nameless, lonely grave. A slow, sadistic death to which he had consigned her almost casually. Vlota knew that her hunger to amply repay him had kept her alive even after every hope was gone, and the will to live itself had abandoned her.

So she cherished her revenge for the ally it had been in her time of greatest need. She would allow no one to prevent its luscious fulfillment.

The M–80 barrage covered the muzzle blasts from the Heckler and Koch P7 automatic as she steadied it with both of her strong, black-gloved hands. Even at a range of twenty feet, aiming was difficult in the swirling murk that Paine had created to mask his flight. As much as she hated him, she found herself admiring his style. The strain of keeping him under constant surveillance unassisted was also telling on her. But that burden was essential to the duel taking place between them. They were both isolated and completely on their own. His comrades had turned on him; hers were an ocean and a continent away. It was just the two of them... they would have to stand or fall on the strength of their individual resources alone... dancing the dance of death at a distance, until the music ended, for one of them or both.

Though the conditions were less than ideal, Vlota was able to put three nine-millimeter slugs into the back of each agent before she returned the compact handgun to the pocket of her black jacket. Then she retreated down the alley into the concealment provided by a massive trash container.

Seconds later, Paine let go of the ladder and dropped agilely onto the chest of one of the fresh government corpses.

Without thought, as he threw himself away from the body, he snatched the .357 from his waistband, aimed, and was squeezing the trigger before he was able to check the reaction. He froze where he was, poised on the balls of his feet, with one hand pressed against the pavement for support, and tried to make sense of what he beheld.

He'd seen enough of them over the years to know new stiffs when he saw them. Voices and vehicles were approaching through the smoke from every direction. He had to be on his way.

He headed west, up the alley, toward Lexington and Park Avenues, darting from doorway to doorway with the gun held at the ready.

It was Bill Mitchell all over again, Paine realized.

Two more deaths would now be added to his bogus list of victims.

Someone had killed to keep him free again.

A jealous presence with whom he shared the night.

As he moved, Martina Vlota stuck with him. As inescapable as the memory of malice.

6

"Your sidekick killed two Bureau agents last night," Berghold said. "He tried to parboil a building full of sleeping civilians at the same time, and nearly succeeded."

The head of Internal Security perched on a corner of his desk in front of Cunningham's wheelchair. His coat was off, his tie loosened. Both had been done consciously moments before the analyst of Soviet intelligence rolled through the office door in response to his summons.

Berghold wanted Cunningham to understand he was being called in for a friendly chat, not a cold-blooded interrogation. Of course, if the kisses and hugs didn't get Berghold the intimacy he was after, gang rape was what Cunningham could expect at their next get-together. He and Paine were thick as thieves. He must know something. If, in truth, he didn't, it might not be a bad time to start pretending.

"I assume you're referring to John Paine?" Kevin Cunningham said. His still youthful, all-American features were typically composed and radiated self-confidence despite his missing limbs. His tone was polite, but there was an edge of irritation to it. Berghold knew that Cunningham was touchy on the subject of his old friend ever since Paine had turned rogue and soared to the top of any wanted list worthy of the name.

"That's right, Kevin," Berghold replied. "I didn't call you in to give you grief about it. I know this whole affair has been a bitch for you since it started. I hate to think how I'd feel if I were in your shoes." Berghold groaned inside and kicked himself for the use of the grindingly inappropriate metaphor. Cunningham, however, seemed not to notice. Berghold assumed he had become inured to such gaffes long before.

"Thanks, Mark. I appreciate your understanding," Cunningham said.

"Nevertheless," Berghold continued, "Paine must be stopped before he does even greater harm. Under the circumstances, your duty to your country must come before any bonds of friendship that might exist."

Berghold expected Cunningham to leap to Paine's defense as he had done repeatedly over the weeks since the East German fiasco. When that reaction was not forthcoming, Berghold had to struggle to stifle his surprise.

"Frankly, Mark, no one has been keeping me current on John's latest crimes. I did hear that he was back in the country, but that only came to me through the Company grapevine. It might be a good idea for you to fill me in on the rest of it," Cunningham said solemnly.

John's latest crimes? Berghold didn't know

what to make of Cunningham's drastic change of opinion regarding his friend.

"I agree," Berghold replied, nodding his assent as he crossed his arms on his chest. "I'll summarize for you his most outstanding felonies since his return."

If Mark Berghold was anything like the judge of human behavior that he believed himself to be, Kevin Cunningham was repeatedly shocked by each new revelation of Paine's homicidal savagery. When the recitation was concluded, the cripple sat there silently staring off into space.

"I have a confession to make, Mark. Something I've been needing to get off my chest for a long time," Cunningham said quietly.

Berghold had to fight back the smile that threatened to expand across his face. Cunningham was coming clean with only a little good-natured urging. Score another victory for cunning over simple brute force. Maybe Cunningham was a traitor, too. And Mark Berghold had personally bagged him. If only he were wired to record it. He cursed his low opinion of his own persuasiveness. No matter. It was too late now. He could not risk breaking the momentum of what Cunningham was about to say. If it was a confession of treason, he would simply have to coax him into repeating it later for the record.

Nixon had been right all along. There were some men who should record absolutely everything.

"Go ahead, Kevin," Berghold said softly, doing his best Spencer Tracy impersonation.

"Ever since the war, I've been afraid that

John was going to lose control someday. I still have nightmares about some of the things we did back then." Cunningham lowered his gaze to the floor and seemed to stare straight through the globe to the steamy jungle world on its other side. "He wasn't the only one who did terrible, unholy things in Nam. I did them, too. And other men we knew. Things that would make you sick if I told you. They bothered me even then. But they didn't bother John. That's how I knew he wouldn't return to normal like the rest of us did when it was over. Because that *was* normal. For him."

Berghold felt the disappointment rising in him. *This* was Cunningham's confession? Another tiresome mea culpa about dark deeds during the war? Who cared? Certainly not Mark Berghold. And he hardly needed more proof that Paine was a homicidal maniac. But if that's all there was to Cunningham's soul baring, at least he was placing himself squarely on the correct side for a change.

"Then you have no trouble believing Paine capable of the things he's done thus far?" Berghold asked.

"Mark, the only trouble I have is believing that John is going to continue to be so *restrained*." Cunningham met Berghold's eyes with his own. "These aren't easy things for me to say. John is and always has been my best friend. I did my utmost to ignore all the evidence against him for as long as I could. I'll never forget that I owe my life to him. Do you have any idea what a debt that is?" he asked.

"Yes, I do," Berghold answered severely,

matching his tone to the subject matter. Doing George C. Scott. In fact, he did not know what it was like, and considered it a maudlin topic for grown men to be discussing.

"It's something you live with every day, the way you live with multiple amputations. You can't ever forget it, even if you might want to very much sometimes. I owe whatever I am to John Paine, but that no longer blinds me to the fact that he's the most violent, dangerous man I've ever met." Cunningham's brow furrowed, and he rubbed it with his remaining hand, as if attempting to smooth his face and his mind at the same time. "Anyone who gets on his list has my sympathy. Because they just ran out of luck."

Cunningham was tailoring the truth to give himself better standing with the Company, as John Paine had suggested. In the best tradition of deception throughout the ages, he was leaving the facts basically alone, only adding a minor lie here and there as spice. The overall effect was to change the "flavor" of reality while leaving its contents almost unchanged.

As any student of mendacity knew, among the singular advantages of this approach was the ease with which the lie could be delivered, being couched as it was in the midst of a bed of truth. Cunningham radiated sincerity without much effort. He and Paine *had* done atrocious things during the war. He *had* recognized the difference between Paine and most other men early on. Paine *was* dangerous both by inclination and experience.

But he was giving Berghold the impression

that he was on the Agency's side; that he now believed his friend had gone bad and was wasting his former colleagues right and left for the sheer animal pleasure it afforded him. That was not the way it was. Kevin Cunningham knew John Paine was trapped in a taut web of intrigue that left him no choice but to act as he was acting if he wanted to stay alive. Cunningham understood the nature of the game far better than Berghold, better even than Paine himself. He was in a better position to understand than almost anyone. Life as a triple amputee had taught him the fine arts of observation and analysis better than a person who was whole could ever learn them. Participation in most normal activities was denied him. He had vast quantities of time and energy to devote to studying things from the sidelines, and he took full advantage of them. He had discovered his studious side in college, where his mentors had led him to understand the world and himself far better than he ever had before. Since his recruitment by the Company upon graduation, he had discovered a part of himself that thrived on the shadow world of espionage.

No one, not even John Paine, knew how devious he could be after so many years spent among spies. It was a side of himself that he kept hidden even as he nurtured it and watched it grow. It amused Cunningham that Berghold thought he was on top of their little meeting... or anything else, for that matter.

He found the job of leading the head of Internal Security astray to be child's play at best.

"I get the impression you think that applies

to you as much as to anyone else," Berghold said. It was a leading question, intended as much to persuade as to inquire. The closer to zero the number of people whom Paine could call friend, the easier it would be for Berghold to sleep until the man was as dead as anyone could ever get.

Cunningham didn't answer immediately. It seemed as if he hadn't faced that particular issue until just then. From what Berghold could tell, the conclusion Cunningham was coming to was not the sort likely to make him rest more comfortably, either.

"To be straight with you, Mark, I guess I've been avoiding asking myself that until now," Cunningham replied, his expression equal parts sadness and unease. "I'm afraid the answer is yes. I'd have to say I think I would be in serious danger if John believed, for whatever reason, that I'd turned on him. I might even have more to fear than most. John approaches friendship like a religion. For him, betraying a friend is a form of heresy."

"Perhaps I should assign some men to you to make sure you don't get burned at the stake. I believe that is the traditional punishment for heretics." Berghold kept his face scrupulously neutral as he eagerly plunged a dagger of fear into Kevin Cunningham's heart.

Cunningham was impressed by Berghold's agile seizure of the slight opening the moment it appeared. It suggested more intelligence than Cunningham thought he possessed. Having admitted to feeling in danger, he couldn't refuse the surveillance without appearing to contradict himself. If he accepted it, the agents who had already been watching him for some time wouldn't have to hide it from him anymore. That would make it much easier for them to stay close to him, and, consequently, much harder for Cunningham and Paine to contact one another without detection.

Even with the change of circumstances, Cunningham knew his friend was equal to the challenge. The worst that was likely to happen was not to Paine, but to any of those watching Cunningham who had the misfortune to be in the wrong place, at the wrong time, with the wrong man.

"Maybe you should, Mark. Not that anything's going to happen," Cunningham said, injecting the proper note of false courage in his reply.

"No," Berghold said, "I'm sure it's not. But I'll give you a shadow as insurance. And as a token of my esteem." Berghold stood up and offered his smile and his hand to the man in the wheelchair. It was his way of saying that Cunningham was dismissed, and implying that the cripple had passed his test with high marks. They both knew Berghold reserved almost all of his esteem for himself.

"An esteem, Mark, that I return with interest," Cunningham responded. They both also knew that Cunningham had no more respect for the head of Internal Security than did anyone else in the Company. But respect was not the real issue. Intimidation was, and Cunningham made the obligatory gesture to assure Berghold he was overjoyed to survive the encounter with all his skin in place.

On his way back to his office, Kevin Cunningham was pleased with the way it had gone. And, as he tightened his tie and slipped his coat back on, Mark Berghold was pleased, too.

"I must be getting sloppy in my declining years," Paine said. He was huddled on the floor in the back of Cunningham's sedan. Earlier in the day, he had left a message with his friend's secretary that a "Mr. Wellington" wanted to speak with him. Then he had hung up the phone in the booth from which he'd called.

It was their prearranged signal for meeting according to a plan they had devised. At the end of the day, Cunningham had waited his usual hour to let the D.C. rush hour traffic subside. Then he'd driven off the grounds at Langley, taking his usual route home. Along the way, however, he'd exited the freeway for a side trip at one of the local malls.

By the time he parked in the location they had selected, Cunningham had spotted his tail. Berghold was wasting no time delivering on his generous promise of close "protection." The two agents in the generic four-door from the motor pool were not laying back to maintain a buffer of traffic between them. They were acting more like an open escort. Cunningham wondered if, as a result, the contact might not be blown.

For an hour he motored around the mall, inviting the usual gawks and expressions of pity that normally kept him away from such public places. Cunningham had adjusted about as well as any man could to his condition, but it galled him every day of his life, appearances to the contrary notwithstanding. He had started out in life as a whole man, and he would go to his grave wanting to be one again. He found coping with his cursed status as little more than a mobile torso hard enough without being examined like one of the featured attractions at the county fair.

The two-headed dog. The snake woman. The partial man.

The rolling war memorial.

He purchased several items, knowing his every move was being noted for later communication to Berghold, before he returned to his car, and his chaperons returned to theirs, which was parked a polite, if obvious, distance away.

John Paine was sandwiched out of sight, waiting for him, when Cunningham laboriously fitted himself and the chair into the vehicle.

They waited until they were out of the garage, cruising smoothly in the deepening twilight, with the tail an unvarying block behind them before they started talking.

"You're still as good as you ever were, John," Cunningham replied. "But even you aren't invisible. I don't know how you can remain active and survive with so many people looking for you."

Paine filled him in on the way it had been the night before. How close.

"Berghold said you killed two agents," Cunningham said.

"Someone did. I can vouch for that. It was another setup like the one with Mitchell in Paris," Paine said grimly.

"They died because they got in the way?" Cunningham had to resist the impulse to turn his head when he spoke.

"That's right," Paine responded. "They might have had me otherwise. I don't think whoever it is cares who gets the blame as long as I remain in play."

"Sounds pretty twisted to me," Cunningham said.

"Very twisted, and very skilled. My shadow took advantage of the diversion I created to waste them so that I wouldn't be alerted to his presence. He's probably tailing the goons who are tailing you. The man is good," Paine said.

"The word is out that you've graduated to mass murder after the fire you set," Cunningham said, trying to study his mirror closely without being obvious about it.

"Sure thing. My guess is they put it out before it got the job done on my flat. New York firefighters are the best in the world. How did it go between you and Berghold?" Paine squirmed in the cramped space, doing his best to lessen his discomfort. The space between the seats was too much like a straitjacket for his liking.

"I think I convinced him that I've seen the light. You should have been there. You would have enjoyed it," Cunningham said with a smile.

"Believe me, if I had been there, *Berghold* wouldn't have enjoyed it," Paine said. He knew the head of Internal Security was the man in charge of his prompt termination. Paine was looking forward to having a heart-to-heart with Berghold about that as soon as it could be arranged.

"To say the least. He does his best not to show it, but Berghold needs a change of skivvies every time he thinks of you. I assured him that having Jack the Ripper for a pal affected me in much the same way. I could tell that made him feel better. You probably noticed he offered me surveillance to ease my pain, and I had to accept to keep my change of heart looking sincere," Cunningham said.

"Yes. I noticed. I wish those morons were the worst of my problems. How are you doing on getting me the codes?" Paine asked.

At that, Cunningham hazarded a glance over his shoulder at Paine. "I'm sorry, John. Since your return, security has been doubled almost daily at Langley. There's a real siege mentality in place there. I've never seen anything like it. It's a paranoic's delight."

"I *have* to have those codes, Kevin. I'm certain I can determine who the mole is once I have access to the individual dossiers of those I suspect. Without the means to penetrate Octopus, I could be out here in the cold forever. You know that." The flint in Paine's voice left no room for doubt of his commitment to unmasking his deadly foe.

"Of *course* I know it, John," Cunningham replied. "I'm on your side, remember? The codes are only available now on a need-to-know basis. Every request has to go through Rafferty personally. I can't go in and tell him I'd like to take a stroll through the files for the hell of it. I have to have a solid reason. One that he'll buy. And so far I haven't come up with one. You're not the only one who has to keep a low profile, all right?"

"Okay. I'm not telling you to hang yourself. It's just that time is on the mole's side, and he knows it. Sooner or later I'm bound to run out of luck. All he has to do is remain hidden until then. Once I'm on ice, his worries are over. I have to find him and cash him out before someone does the same to me," Paine said heatedly.

Although Paine was sincere about the codes and the background reports he could access by using them, he wasn't as certain as he professed to be about how much they would reveal. Paine realized the mole had probably anticipated such a search far in advance. Whoever had recruited the mole had no doubt foreseen it as well. It was of the nature of such lengthy intrigues that every precaution was taken to make the mole's background look good enough to stand up to even the most suspicious scrutiny.

It was simply an available opportunity that must be explored. The only thing Paine knew for sure was that he must keep the pressure on in every way he could dream up.

"I know your life is on the line, John. I'll keep looking for a way to get the codes. You have my word on that," Cunningham said. He signaled for the exit from the freeway that would take him to his neighborhood and his home.

"Good enough," Paine said.

"Where are you going to be staying now?"

Cunningham asked as he took the ramp that led down to a boulevard.

"I don't know for sure. Maybe with a lady who made me an offer a few days back," Paine said, thinking of the brash businesswoman on the jumbo he'd left abruptly at Kennedy. If he sought her out, it would be against his better judgment. For the time being, he knew, he was better off alone. He was unlikely to bring anything but grief to anyone he touched. But he'd been doing without for too long. Without passion. Without warmth. Without someone in whom he could confide. Even a man like himself needed such things occasionally if he was to remain alive inside. Maybe she could provide them. Maybe it could be done without either of them getting hurt in the process. But Paine seriously doubted that.

"How will I get in touch with you if I get the codes?" Cunningham asked.

"I'll let you know."

"Okay, but don't take too long. Remember, we're a team these days," Cunningham said, noting with a glance that their tail had dropped to two blocks behind in the lighter suburban traffic.

"I'll remember. Before I return to New York, I have some work to do here," Paine said. There was a hint of malicious mirth in his tone.

"You're not going to do anything I'll be sorry for, are you, John?"

"Don't sweat it, Kevin. I have a valentine to deliver to one of our friends in the Company. That's all." This time Paine's amusement was even more apparent.

"I don't think I like whatever it is you have planned, amigo," Cunningham replied anxiously.

"I don't think he's going to like it very much, either," Paine said. "Is there some place around here where you can pull in and get out of sight long enough for me to bail out?"

"There's a fast-food joint up ahead with a drive-through. Will that do?" Cunningham checked his mirror again. The tail was still two blocks behind.

"It'll do fine. Whip around the building. As soon as you hit the brakes, I'll be on my way." Paine turned his large frame with difficulty until he was poised facing the door.

"All right." When the sedan reached the entrance to the restaurant, Cunningham swerved into the lot without slowing. Racing maneuvers that had to be executed with only one hand to manipulate the modified controls were a challenge, but Cunningham pulled it off with both room and time to spare. He braked suddenly the moment the building was between them and the surveillance team.

"Stay healthy, John," Cunningham called as he turned toward the opening door.

"I will, or die trying," Paine shot back with a smile. Then he was out, slamming the door behind him, and vaulting the high screening fence a few feet away with the agility of a man half his age and size.

Cunningham was ordering a double cheese with fries when his escorts appeared behind him once again.

7

"Who's the best contract agent in the business?" Berghold asked Norman Sotus, his new second-in-command.

"Posey is the best, sir," Sotus replied. He was the only man at Langley with a flattop haircut. In combination with the scar that sliced diagonally across his face, it gave him an air that was at once rugged and anachronistic. Sotus liked people to assume the scar was earned when he served with the Third Marines during the war. In fact, he acquired it while flying through a windshield in Santa Monica shortly after his return.

"How soon could you get him here?" Berghold asked.

"Not for some time, sir, I don't think. He's busy killing Zulus for the South African Defense Force. To my knowledge, it's a long-term commitment," Sotus said with an apologetic shake of his bristling gray head.

"Who's second best?" Berghold kept his attention on the matter in hand as he spoke, in keeping with his lifelong aversion to getting it caught in his zipper.

"That would be Samson, sir," Sotus responded. He kept his eyes on his superior, who stood three urinals down to his left.

"Is he available for an assignment at the moment?" Berghold asked on his way to the basin to wash his hands.

"Yes, sir. I think he is," Sotus said, following a few steps behind him.

"How long has it been since he worked for us?" Berghold said.

"About three years, if I recall correctly," Sotus answered while squirting soap into his palm.

"Why so long?" Berghold said.

"Price, mainly, I'd say," Sotus remarked as he worked up a lather. "He's very high. Six figures, at least."

"I know that," Berghold replied curtly as he rinsed the soap from his hand. "They all rob as well as they kill. You say, price *mainly*. What's the rest of it?"

"He's been known to get carried away with his work," Sotus said. He was looking pointedly at Berghold when Berghold glanced at him from where he stood beside the air dryer.

"Too much of a taste for it?" Berghold said.

"He's not always neat," Sotus replied obliquely. It was the conventional description of one who was not above wholesale slaughter on the way to his goal.

"Nevertheless ... it's too late to quibble over price or method with regard to the termination of John Paine. Do whatever is required to get in touch with Samson. Arrange a meeting with him as soon as possible. I'll deal with him personally on this," Berghold concluded, taking a moment to check his appearance in the mirror before turning toward the door. "Did I say something amusing?" Berghold chanced to catch a glimpse of a smirk passing like a wind-driven shadow across his lieutenant's coarse lips.

"No, sir. It's just that you've never met Samson before, have you?" Sotus asked with a perverse twinkle in his pale brown eyes.

"No. I haven't. So what?"

"Samson is nuts. He makes your skin crawl. Hardly anybody wants to meet him twice. That's all," Sotus said with a shrug.

"Great," Berghold replied with disgust. "A new loony to send after the one we lost."

"With all due respect, sir. Samson and Paine aren't even in the same ballpark. Compared to Samson, Paine is a model of mental health," Sotus said.

The next morning...

In the three-car garage of George Rafferty's stately Georgian home...

The two rookie agents assigned to overseeing Rafferty's safety from dawn to dusk had just come on duty. Both were single, and Washington (where eligible males like themselves were outnumbered two-to-one by toothsome young women, three-to-one if the merely eager and adequate were taken into account) was a draining habitat for those who were not opposed to the pleasures of the flesh.

As it so happened, not only was neither opposed, both were ardent advocates of the same.

Actual uninterrupted sleep was a thing they reminisced about on occasion, taking comfort in the mutual conviction that it might be an ordeal, but someone had to take up the slack for all the fags with which the nation's capital was infested.

They took their time, going through all the standard, practiced motions of sweeping the garage for any threats to their charge's well-being, expecting to find nothing.

"So I told her, 'Relax, baby. It's not that I'm too big. You're just tense, is all. Go with the flow. A woman needs to expand to meet new opportunities.' Great line, huh?" He lit a cigarette, picking at the granules left in his eyes by the brief slumber he'd been able to grab.

"Yeah. The stuff of genius. You're so full of it, you waddle. Did you know that?" The other agent stretched like a tall, tailored house cat, wondering how well off you had to be to own a Mercedes, a Porsche, *and* a Jag. "Where did you say you snagged this beast?"

"At Solo's. It was ladies' night," he said, casually waving the long metal wand with the mirror on the end under the gas tank of the Mercedes.

"There hasn't been a lady in that dive since the place opened," his colleague responded.

"Yeah. Thank God." As he kept up the patter, he kept his eyes fixed on the reflection of the car's undercarriage. It required little of his attention. He considered it a job better suited to a trained monkey.

"I'm taking tonight off. I had trouble remembering where I lived this morning," the other said.

"Good idea. A man like you has to pace himself if he's going to keep rising to the occasion. Me, I just plug myself into my cigarette lighter on the way to work. It only takes me about ten minutes to recharge," he said, stepping around to the side of the car and squatting to run the mirror under the transmission.

"I'd better get myself one of those attachments. Sounds real convenient." He leaned against the wall, watching his partner work, feeling no remorse. They alternated on the cars. He would be doing the Porsche next.

"Yeah. You *wish* you had my attachment. Then you'd learn what popularity's all about!" He raised his voice, smirking wearily, in order to be heard on the other side of the car.

Then the smirk was guillotined by what he beheld.

"Whoa," he said. "Stop your grinnin' and drop your linen! Look at what we have here!"

The other agent was beside him in seconds.

"Bingo. Looks like Semtex to me. What do you think?" The mirror's reflection revealed an electronic option wired into the electrical system of the Benz that had not come as standard equipment. It was rectangular in shape with multicolored wires protruding from both ends. The body of the rectangle was composed of what looked like a smooth layer of caramel that had been molded to the mechanism beneath it.

Semtex was the state-of-the-art plastic explosive made in Czechoslovakia that had been in vogue for some time. It didn't show up on sniffers; it was reassuringly stable; and a few ounces was sufficient to blow the hell out of just about anything.

The two knew if the substance was Semtex, there was more than enough to put them, the three cars, and the garage itself into earth orbit.

"I think we'd better call the bomb squad," his partner said respectfully. "There's no telling how many ways the thing may be rigged to blow. Not if Paine put it there. Don't touch the car. It might have a temblor switch on it." Temblor switches responded to the slightest vibration.

"How in the hell did he get in here last night?"

"The sucker must be smoother than smoke. I'm glad he's not after my butt. I'll make the call." He rose and moved briskly toward the wall phone to summon the specialists.

His partner remained crouched next to the Mercedes, studying the bomb in the mirror.

"There's something unnatural about that guy. I think we need a priest."

It required the entire morning for the specialists to cautiously determine that the bomb was a fake. A fake insofar as the malleable substance that resembled Semtex turned out to be nothing more destructive than modeling clay. In all other respects, however, the device was the genuine item, rigged in the prescribed fashion, to detonate when any one of its four separate switches was activated. None of the men who removed it discounted the way it had been placed in plain sight beneath the vehicle. It could just as easily have been artfully concealed. Had that been the case and had Semtex been the explosive, it would have gone unnoticed until George Rafferty and his earthly cares became one with the atoms of his Benz in a single volcanic moment.

When the modeling clay was peeled away from the apparatus, there was a neatly printed note inside. The note was immediately rushed to Langley on Rafferty's order, and no mention was made to Brock of anything regarding the incident. Since his abduction by Paine, the Director had been flying into fits of rage at the very mention of the rogue agent. Rafferty privately feared Brock was courting a breakdown if Paine wasn't run to ground in short order.

After he read the note, Rafferty held it between his hands for some minutes, simply staring at it.

The note read:

Dear George,

Like your boss, I had you if I wanted you, and I let you go. Would I have done that if I were the man you take me to be? I think not. There is little to fear from a snake if you remove its head, is there? We both understand that principle. I have allowed the snake to live because I am not the traitor that you seek. You are wasting your time chasing me. This is exactly what our mutual enemy wants you to do. Someone got to Wilson and convinced him I was dirty. Who was in a position to do that? You're a smart man, George. Isn't it time you started acting like one?

                                        Paine.

The more Rafferty thought about it, the worse it bothered him. If Paine *was* a psycho and a turncoat, why hadn't he simply murdered both of them when he had the chance? It wasn't all that much of a stretch to come up with a lunatic justification for it after all the bad blood that had developed between the two of them and the assassin. And their deaths would have dealt a massive blow to the country's intelligence community, thereby severely reducing its effectiveness for an indefinite period. Any country to which Paine might have switched his allegiance would be overjoyed by such a development. Even including, arguably, some of America's titular allies. So if the operative had, in fact, gone bad for one reason or the other, why was he going to such baroque lengths to prove that he had not?

Granted, in the realm of clandestine affairs, *nothing* was ever what it appeared to be on the surface. But wasn't it possible they *were* all being taken, collectively, for a ride? If that was true, and the Company had been nudged onto the wrong road at the start, then all they were doing was laying waste to the countryside to prove their original assumption had been right.

Rafferty was appalled by the possibility that they might have been engaging in a marathon burlesque of self-deception. He vowed to follow Paine's suggestion and return to the starting point to reexamine all that had happened as objectively as possible, unburdened by the bonds of preconception that had thus far hobbled all of them.

* * *

"I have only a few brief questions for you, Cunningham. Then you can return to whatever it is you're working on," Rafferty said as the man rolled across the carpet to his desk.

Rafferty was not a man to delay when he believed something needed to be done. It was only two hours since Paine's note had reached his desk. He had acquired, in that time, a list of all personnel with whom Wilson had been acquainted. He was methodically working his way down that list alphabetically, personally interviewing each and every one.

"We're presently collating a raft of fresh intercepts from Big Daddy, sir," Cunningham said. Big Daddy was that great thief of global communications, the National Security Agency.

"Since we're both very busy, I'll get straight to the point. How well did you know the man Wilson, who died under disputed circumstances while on a mission with your friend Paine in East Germany?" George Rafferty asked the question conversationally, but his eyes missed nothing.

"Not very well, actually. We worked together on a couple of projects some time back. Occasionally we would find ourselves tipping a few with the usual bunch of guys at the local watering hole. That's about it," Cunningham said.

"Do you recall anyone in the organization he was especially close to? Someone who might be more than just a casual acquaintance?" Rafferty asked.

Cunningham deliberated a few moments before he responded.

"No, offhand I can't say that I do. I'm afraid I can't be very helpful regarding Wilson, sir. He had his life. I had mine. It was only at rare intervals that we even crossed paths."

"All right. That's all. You can return to your work now. Sorry about the interruption." Rafferty nodded his thanks, but appeared too preoccupied to even notice when Cunningham responded, rotated the chair, and rolled out of the room, leaving the smell of hot oil in his wake.

As he made his way back to his office, Kevin Cunningham didn't know what to make of it. He'd assumed the whole matter of Wilson's death and who was responsible for it to have been decided and set in stone. Did Rafferty's questions mean it was being reopened? If so, did that mean that the issue of Paine's loyalty was being reconsidered, too?

Did any of that matter if Lucian Brock had decreed that he should die?

When he reached his desk, Cunningham's body was there, but his mind was somewhere else for the remainder of the afternoon.

8

The phone was answered on the sixth ring.
"Hello," she said.
"Hello."
Pause.
"Who is this?" she asked.
"It's the jumper," he replied deeply.
Pause.
"Is this an obscene phone call?" She sounded amused, if somewhat blasé.
"Could you use one?" His voice was somewhat familiar, and the kind of sleek baritone she favored.
Pause.
"Come to think of it, it might hit the spot," she answered archly.
"In a manner of speaking," he responded.
"But it all depends," she rejoined tentatively.
"On what?" he inquired.
"On whether or not you're good at it," she said.
"Good at what?" he asked.
"At the whole heavy-breathing routine. You

know. All the gross anatomical terms and vivid descriptions of all the lewd torment you'd like to put me through," she said briskly.

"I think I can handle it. But your anatomy didn't look all that gross to me," he said deferentially.

"You're the dashing character from the plane, aren't you?" she said with an ill-concealed note of wonder and delight.

"The same. You're as quick as you seemed," Paine replied.

"Are all your conquests achieved with such élan?" she asked.

"Invariably. It's essential to my mystique," he said simply.

"You certainly know how to disturb people in droves," she remarked with an admiring smile he could not see.

"Do I disturb you?" Paine asked.

"Intensely," she purred, stressing the central syllable.

"Would you like me to disturb you some more?" Paine asked softly.

"At great length, hopefully," she purred some more.

The address she gave him was on Central Park West, a few blocks north of Columbus Circle. The location was further evidence that, whatever the woman did to earn her bread, she did it well enough to cart the stuff home in trucks. Her building was a high-rise condominium, as pricey as everything else in the vicinity.

He entered Central Park by way of the

Ninety-sixth Street Transverse shortly after 10:00 P.M. on a Friday night. The brilliance and bustle of Park Avenue soon diminished behind him as he strode lightly toward the reservoir. The darkness and the lingering warmth of the day were a sea in which he swam with ease. Like a thing that claimed the top of the food chain as its right and natural position.

The way he moved was a statement of his disinterest in the park's fearsome nocturnal reputation; the way he looked was like one of those denizens upon which that reputation was founded. As he proceeded on a general southwest diagonal, Paine stopped occasionally for minutes at a time; doubled back on his path; employed every technique he knew to disconnect from any possible pursuer.

He took his time, using the park and its pitfalls as a seine with which to snare the perpetual shadow he had thus far been unable to shake. Perhaps a mugger or some less savory brand of thug would succeed where he had failed. In that event, his only regret would be not having a ringside seat from which to enjoy the match. Paine suspected, however, that such a contest was more inclined to spell the end of the thug than that of his nemesis. But he was willing to settle for enough in the way of interference to sever the bond between himself and his lethal Siamese twin.

Paine knew he must be one of the few people in Manhattan who found the heart of Central Park captivating when it was pumping the black blood of the night. One of the few sane ones, at least. The towering trees, the plazas, the monuments, all called to something deep within him like the grand terrain of some lost world which he, alone, inhabited. It brought to mind other such places that he loved... the Bois de Boulogne in Paris... St. James Wood in London... the Acropolis in Athens. There was something about each after nightfall that evoked visions of apocalypse in him, an end-of-the-world atmosphere that he relished.

The weird ambiance of the park was enhanced by the gleaming towers that flanked almost its entire circumference. The contrast between their brilliant order and the rolling onyx miles of the wooded, rocky chaos they confined was striking in its extremity.

As he approached the lights and the traffic of Central Park West, Paine was reluctant to leave the brutal simplicity of the park behind. Compared to the teeming metropolis all around, its dangers were obvious. They made no pretense of being anything but what they were. They did not smile and seduce with a dagger held, poised to strike, behind their backs. They were open threats that announced their intentions well in advance.

Though his life was founded on deceit, John Paine preferred a more sincere sort of savagery. It was in the open arena that he functioned best. He had practiced duplicity for so long that it had become second nature to him. Never, however, had it ceased to be a chore. And he knew that if Death ever managed to claim him as he practiced his trade, it would do so in the form of treachery.

His thoughts revolved around betrayal as he

strutted out of the woods, sneering belligerently at the cop behind the wheel of a blue-and-white trolling slowly past, headed south toward midtown. He was attired in a manner that would have drawn attention in the hinterland, but deflected it in the Big Apple's jaded core. The cop gave him no more than a brief, bored glance before looking elsewhere.

Why, Paine wondered, had the woman been so forward about making his acquaintance? She was certainly sharp enough to realize he was in serious trouble with serious people, and lots of them. Why didn't her common sense dictate she should pursue her amusement with someone who wasn't on the run? A woman with her looks and brains and bucks would be anything but starved for worthy male attention. All the malarkey about good men being hard to find notwithstanding.

The message she'd been broadcasting thus far said that he was simply irresistible. In Paine's opinion, there were only a couple of problems with that. First, it wasn't true. Desirable, maybe. But there was a long distance between "worth looking into" and "can't keep my eyes off of you." Movie stars were irresistible. John Paine was not a movie star, and would never be one.

Second, it played too blatantly to his ego.

His was a profession in which you soon learned that no one acted worshipful unless they took you for a fool. Strokes were only administered as a sedative to your defenses. If you had a weakness for praise, it would be discovered, and honeyed words would be used to put you in a trance from which you might never recover.

Paine knew an insatiable ego was as fatal an addiction for an operative as a hunger for money or drugs. And even a normal ego could be intoxicated by the adulation of some delicacy of whichever gender a given individual might prefer. In the game he played, seduction was a more common weapon than handguns. And one that was more reliably accurate and final.

There was even a slang term to cover it... sexpionage. The word was a recent coinage, but the practice it referred to was as old as the game itself, possibly older. There were terms, too, for those who specialized in sexual subversion. The women were "sparrows"; the men, "ravens." In the amoral, ruthless world in which they functioned, it was understood that the conventional distinction between "hetero" and "homosexual" preferences did not apply. Sparrows and ravens bedded men and women alike, with equal expertise and abandon. Any vestiges of such quaint inhibitions were burned out of them at the start of their training with merciless premeditation. Such agents were molded into equal-opportunity, all-purpose whores whose inclinations were suited to all partners and every conceivable occasion, from the most demure to the most obscene.

Paine knew that some of them were as adept in their own way as he was in his, and he respected them accordingly.

Was this confident, engaging female, whose name he still did not know, a sparrow? To be on the safe side, Paine considered it probable.

It was, however, what the lawyers would call a "rebuttable presumption," meaning she could change his opinion by offering the proper evidence to the contrary. But even if she didn't, he was not averse to screwing a sparrow, to put it rudely, under the appropriate circumstances, which he deemed these to be.

Paine knew, with all due modesty, that he was likely to be far better at covering himself than she would be at uncovering him. His track record demonstrated that conclusively. If anything, the ramparts he had erected over the years to secure his safety from every possible form of attack were too high and wide. Paine possessed sufficient insight to realize that he dwelt within a fortress so vast and impregnable that even someone who wished him well could not penetrate it to reach him. And he was wise enough to know the fate of those who steeped themselves in solitude for too long.

So he was more curious than concerned about the woman. The maxim in the trade held, in matters sexual, that the likelihood of the interest being genuine was inversely proportional to the allure of the individual displaying it. If that was true, it was not impossible that the lady was for real, but it was nothing to bet the house on, either.

He entered the building by the locked service door in the rear after reconnoitering the block for half an hour. The stairs took him to her floor, the twelfth, unobserved. All the appointments of the place were suitably tasteful and subdued. It reminded Paine of some of the more elegant hotels he'd inhabited in the States and in Europe, as well. The carpet in her hall looked like it belonged on the wall. Between the electric candles in their gilt sconces affixed to polished marble of a rich blue-green.

Since he'd entered, the air around him had been thick with a solid quiet that seemed to gulp even the slightest sound at birth. He didn't know the names of the colors that were used, but "mauve" and "puce" came to mind. He thought of them as "snooty" shades. Exercises in self-conscious good taste.

The woman who promptly answered his knock, however, was anything but. He was favorably impressed as a result.

She was wearing a flannel shirt tucked into pleated corduroy slacks. Both were oversized in the name of comfort. Her petite figure was nearly lost in them, but there were hints, here and there, of wonders lurking among the folds. Her feet were clad in sloppy moccasins over loud argyles. All in all, she reminded him of a walking advertisement for L. L. Bean. He liked that.

Given the ritzy setting she had chosen to call home, she seemed to be a woman with a taste for luxury who refused to kneel before the throne of style. One who knew the difference between possessing the finer things, and being possessed by them.

He, on the other hand, resembled nothing more than a surly, swaggering, and soiled specimen of hopeless biker trash. A large, faded bandanna was pulled tight over his head, knotted in the back, with tails that hung to the middle of his back. The black leather jacket, blue jeans, and engineer boots didn't look like they needed an occupant to help them move from place to place. Cheap black plastic sunglasses and a toothpick in the corner of his mouth served as perfect fashion accents to the ensemble.

"Halloween either came early this year, or I just opened the door for the wrong dude," she said with an expression of wry amusement as she looked him up and down. "Tell me you're the jumper...please."

"Relax," Paine said. "I only dress like this to fool my fans. Otherwise, they hound me unmercifully. May I come in?"

"By all means. I wouldn't have it any other way." Her look of amusement broadened as she stepped back out of his way.

Paine gave her a smile of his own in return. He hadn't known what to expect when she opened the door, given the unorthodox nature of their "courtship" to date. He was relieved that she hadn't greeted him in a black lace teddy, studded dog collar, and ice-pick heels. In New York, among other such seats of outrage, a man never knew how aggressive an aggressive woman might get.

If she had appeared looking like Dracula's daughter in severe need of a few hot pints, it would have been too much of a good thing for Paine's taste, possessing all the earmarks of a glandular ambush from the start. It would also have set a different tone for the hours ahead from the one he had in mind. He was feeling more inclined toward conversation than copulation, for openers at least, and her choice of apparel had left that option as open and available as the look on her slender, pleasant face.

"My name is Constance Schwinn, by the way, and I'll let you know up front that I may be crazy enough to pursue this thing with you, but that doesn't mean I'll tolerate any bicycle jokes when we are together. Understood?" After she closed the door, she crossed her arms over her chest, and stood looking at him challengingly with her feet shoulder width apart.

It was understood.

Paine considered it the least he could do, considering the tissue of lies he was about to spread out before her.

He introduced himself as Neal Heck before she offered to give him the grand tour, and he accepted. Her home impressed him as an accurate reflection of the woman herself: classy without being pretentious; controlled, but not unduly so. Books and music and video fare abounded. So did enough muscular potted plants to create the atmosphere of a well-tended garden throughout.

One bedroom had been transformed into a well-appointed office. Paine had only a passing acquaintance with computers, but he knew enough to identify hers as something far beyond the comparative toys that were becoming almost as common as VCRs. She told him she was a commodities broker who worked as much at home as not. He didn't know what that was; did not care; and doubted he ever would.

While they shared the magnificent view of the park and the twinkling phalanx of vintage skyscrapers along Park Avenue, she got around to asking him who he was and what had made him so unpopular of late. Paine found himself inclined to tell her the essence of the truth. It never occurred to him to do so without altering all the pertinent details by using one of the several cover stories he always kept handy.

That wasn't done. Not even with mothers and wives, let alone with lovers and flings. Such pretense was as reflexive in a field agent as balance was to a dancer. One learned in the beginning that there was no future to look forward to without it. Eventually there was no need to give it thought and no possibility of acting in any other way.

"I shouldn't be here. Coming here has placed you in jeopardy. I'm a free-lance journalist. I was digging up information on neofascists in Germany when they evidently decided I had learned too much," Paine said. He sat facing her on a love seat in her living room. Her reflective blue eyes were fixed on him, surrounded by an expression that was replete with belief and concern.

It didn't trouble Paine that she was offering him a number of valuable things for which he was going to reward her with counterfeit currency. He no longer had qualms about who he was or the way he lived his life. He had survived through connivance and manipulation too long for that. Whatever pangs of conscience he might have experienced in his youth in that regard had faded to nothing more than blurry memories.

"And you knew they might be waiting for you when you entered the terminal at Kennedy...?" Constance said, lifting one stockinged foot up onto the cushion and hugging that knee to her chest.

"The people I upset are not a bunch of goose-stepping morons. They are smart and secretive. They have their sights set much higher than establishing themselves as public nuisances. But that doesn't mean they're not fanatics, or that they won't gladly kill anyone who threatens to expose them," Paine said. He'd removed most of his disguise, stripping down to his tank top and blue jeans. He noticed the way the woman's eyes drifted to his well-muscled torso from time to time, admiring it unabashedly. He knew it was impossible to miss the several scars that were exposed.

"It almost sounds like one of those nerve-jangling movies," she said. "The lone man running for his life from the merciless killers who will stop at nothing to destroy him. Is it as bad as that?" Constance toyed with strands of her boyishly short hair as she awaited his response.

"Yes," Paine said, "I've been in very hot water before, but never anything like this. In my line of work you get used to taking your lumps and going through close scrapes. That isn't the problem. It's that this time I can't see any solution to all of it. Not even in the distance. There's too many of them; too few of me; and no matter what I do, they just keep coming. It's enough to get a man down. Lately I've been running out of steam."

"Are any of these recent?" she asked, reaching over to trace the puckered ridge of a knife scar on his shoulder.

"No," he replied. That was the truth. He hadn't been seriously injured in some time. "They're souvenirs from the war." That was truthful, too, but less so. The "war" he referred to included Vietnam, but was far from limited to it.

"You don't impress me as a journalist," she said as she continued caressing his skin with silky fingertips. "Journalists are observers. Even when they're in the thick of things, most of what they're doing is watching. I get the feeling that when the trouble starts, you're doing a lot more than watching. How did you enter the building without having to buzz me at the front door, by the way?" She nibbled her full lower lip as she looked at him quizzically.

Score one in favor of your being what you say you are, Paine thought as he took a deep whiff of her expensive, body-heated perfume. If the woman was a sparrow, she would be likely to keep such troublesome observations to herself in order to keep their steady slide toward the bedroom as lubricated as possible. Sparrows tended to come off rather dim, in Paine's experience, no matter how quick they were. It was an inevitable by-product of their effort to be constantly accommodating.

As clearly drawn to him as she was, Constance Schwinn was pointing out the cracks in his cover without so much as a second thought. To John Paine, that meant she was either an honest citizen, or a sparrow who was too good to fall prey to the usual mistakes.

"I didn't get into the fix I'm in by being a

typical journalist," Paine replied. Backing up his various cover stories was nothing new to him. He'd had plenty of practice. "As you guessed, I take a far more active approach than most. It includes having learned a good deal about 'B and E' in order to get to information some people would rather keep to themselves."

"'B and E'?" she asked with a slight scowl.

"Breaking and entering," Paine said.

"Oh. So burglary is also among your skills. It gets easier to understand why the people chasing you are so upset." There was admiration in the way she said it. "You think someone might have followed you here?" she asked without apparent fear.

"It's possible," Paine replied with a nod. "Possible enough to make backdoors look a lot better than front doors these days."

"I'm sorry. I forgot to ask if you'd care for a drink. Would you?" She gently closed one hand on his forearm as she asked. Her fingernails were long, but not extremely so, and sculpted. They were painted a shade of tangerine, and matched her lips. Paine found her basic color scheme enticing. The bold splashes on nails and lips were in striking contrast to her milky flesh. The sapphire eyes and shining chocolate mane were equally enhanced by the ivory skin that lent elegance to her slender neck. His eyes were drawn to the generous opening beneath the collar of her shirt, where the first two buttons were left undone.

"A glass of wine would be good," he said. And then, sudden and unexpected, the yawn hit him. He hadn't had more than three hours of sleep in a row for days, and it was telling on him. Paine stretched and flexed, hearing his spine crack as he did, letting the fatigue roll through him. He felt safer and more relaxed than he had for weeks.

When his eyes opened again, Constance Schwinn was kneeling on the love seat beside him, with her delicate hands splayed on her thighs, taking it all in, reminding him of an attentive cat. She looked to Paine like a woman who was enjoying the show, and possibly in the mood to put on a show of her own.

"Are you trying to tell me something?" she asked playfully. "If that's your idea of a good line, then you're even more sure of yourself than I took you to be."

"What it was was an unrehearsed yawn, but if you wanted to interpret it as my way of saying it's time to hit the sack, I wouldn't hold it against you," Paine said with a smile.

"Believe me, sweetheart, if that's the way I interpret it, and I find the idea intriguing, you'd *better* hold it against me." Then, slowly, she leaned toward him, and one hand landed softly on each of his big shoulders. She lowered her face until it was only a few inches from his, holding her slender body poised gracefully above him. "If I weren't such a sophisticated, modern girl, I might consider this a ridiculously brief courtship even for me." She did carnal things with her eyes as she said it, letting them entwine and grow heated with his.

"Were you looking for something more traditional?" Paine asked, knowing the answer.

"With you? I hardly think so," Constance replied, her eyes shining and laughter in her voice.

"I could go out for some flowers," Paine suggested.

"Maybe tomorrow," she said. "Right now we have to conserve your energy." She brought her face even closer, until their lips were nearly touching.

"Why? Do you have something strenuous in mind for me?" he said, laughing softly as he raised both hands and closed them around her small waist.

She grazed his mouth with her own then before she answered. It sent a high-voltage current racing through both of them. They breathed together, and let it build, both knowing the waiting was as good, in its own way, as what came after.

"Don't laugh, Neal. I might be tougher than I look," she said with a chuckle.

Like a number of other pretty ladies in my experience, Paine thought, several of whom I've killed.

"That might make *two* of us," he said, letting his hands roam to wherever they found something interesting to explore.

"I'll bet. But all I really demand is that you be single-minded and ferocious between the sheets," she said between gasps.

"No intellectual stuff, right?" he asked, fondling.

"Brain-dead," she replied with a quiver.

"Goal-oriented and relentless?" Paine was having fun, seeing how long she could keep making sense as his hands became ever more bold.

"All action; no talk. My! You do have the muscles, don't you?" Constance decided it was time to do some exploring of her own. Turnabout was definitely fair play.

"Make me a promise?" Paine asked, believing it was about time to move their conversation to someplace flat and wide and comfortable.

"Name it!" Constance groaned, hyperventilating.

"You'll do the same," he said, fiddling with the buttons of her shirt.

"Consider it done!" she assured him, helping him with the shirt, and then the slacks.

"Do you have Chardonnay?" he asked.

"I think so," Constance said, giggling at the combination of the question and the way she looked. "Would you like some right now?" She was perspiring. There was the ruby mottling of passion on her throat and breast.

"Yes, please," he replied with a smile.

When she struggled to her feet next to the love seat, her shirt fell off and her slacks fell into a pool around her ankles on the floor. She posed there for a moment, letting him inspect her with his eyes. Her matching bra and bikinis were, without question, from some establishment much less woodsy than L. L. Bean.

"I'll only be a moment," she said then as she stepped out of her slacks, pivoted, and hurried off toward the kitchen.

"That's a relief," Paine said.

Five minutes later, with a glass of Chardonnay in each hand, Constance called to him from where she had taken them.

Paine found her reclining on a satin sea, fresh out of talk.

They picked up right where they'd left off.

9

Mark Berghold flew to Costa Rica to interview Samson for the job of removing John Paine from the playing field with all the prejudice that could be arranged.

The location was Samson's idea. He was no more forthcoming about why he favored it than he was about anything else. The Company had evidence, however, that Samson worked as an adviser to the Costa Rican army and security service. As such things went in Central America, there was no sharp distinction between one and the other. It was said that in return for his expertise, Samson received both a fat retainer and the assurance that he would not be extradited, regardless of which nation it was that wanted him or how badly. It was a classical kind of arrangement between such a man and the government that gave him asylum.

There were men who possessed dark knowledge that was extremely valuable in certain quarters. Joseph Mengele, the Death Angel of Auschwitz, had been such a man. For forty years after the fall of the Third Reich, he had parlayed that knowledge into wealthy sanctuary in one South American country after another. Klaus Barbie was another SS monster who'd been clever enough to find work after the war based on an employment history consisting mainly of atrocities. His employer had been the OSS, the parent that bore the CIA in its loins. They'd found the secrets Barbie possessed of greater importance than the legion of French men and women he'd savaged during the Nazi Occupation.

In the intelligence business, expedience frequently dictated pacts with the devil. Such was the nature of the deal between Samson and Costa Rica. It was a marriage with which both were well pleased.

They met in the middle of nowhere, a place that was not difficult to find in Central America in Berghold's opinion. The rendezvous point was a village on the Caribbean coast, a place without a name where tortillas and everything else baked beneath a tropic sun that pounded as relentlessly as the metronomic blue waves.

Samson was squatting in the shade of a palm in front of a picturesque thatched hut when the head of Internal Security for the Company arrived with Norman Sotus. Berghold had led his second-in-command to believe he was bringing him along to fulfill his usual function as a high-level gofer. In reality, Sotus was there to provide moral support. Berghold would have preferred having someone else deal with Samson, but the Paine thing was too far gone for that. There was no leeway remaining even for the delegation of such an unpleasant, not to say fearful, task.

Since his last meeting with the Director, Berghold's sleep had been filled each night with hellish visions of Afghanistan. He was convinced that Brock meant every word about banishing him to that barbarous void where, Berghold assumed, the vulture was the national bird. It was either death for the rogue in the near future, or a living death for Berghold, who would spend the rest of his career fighting body lice and dining on camel casserole.

The Land Rover that met them at the airstrip two hours before churned through the shimmering expanse of beach sand that was as white as virgin snow. The vehicle and its silent Hispanic driver belonged to Samson. When they stopped before the hut, Berghold was still reeling from the beating he'd received along the way. He doubted they had missed a single bone-jarring pothole or obstruction, and suspected the driver had hit them all by design in order to soften the two Company men up for the meeting with his *jefe*.

Berghold's impression of the man in the guayabera shirt waiting for them to come to him where he stood was that Sotus had been right. Samson made your skin want to crawl back home, preferably under the bed. The man was *wrong*. All wrong.

It started with his stature. He was petite. *Petite*. Berghold was tempted to think it was some sort of optical illusion at first, a trick of the stunning sunlight that was reflected from the sand with blinding force. But it was not. The man who had chosen the name of the biblical titan was small, even for a woman. Berghold found himself wishing he had given the killer's dossier more than cursory attention.

It was not until he had entered the shade and advanced close enough for a good look, however, that Berghold appreciated how much more preparation the meeting required. He had known that it would, really, but his instinctive aversion to wetwork and those who practiced it had prevailed over his sense of duty, and he'd simply put it off until he'd conveniently forgotten it.

Berghold had assumed when Sotus referred to Samson's repellant effect on people that the cause was entirely psychological, or very nearly so. But one look at the place where Samson's face had once been located was enough to convince Berghold that the assumption had been as wrong as assumptions usually were.

It was also enough to halt him as abruptly as a man who had walked into a wall.

It was a reaction to which the silent, neat little man was totally accustomed. He had grown to enjoy it over the years since the jerry can of petrol had blown to hell and taken his face with it. He'd been pouring its contents into a jeep at the time, under fire, when a stray tracer had slammed into it. That had been in Angola, where he was employed by the rebels until they ran out of funds or he got a better offer from the other side.

The can had exploded in his hands, creating a small fire storm around his head. There were those who said the intense heat had fried whatever sanity Samson possessed at the time. Though that was subject to debate, the third-degree burns he had received were not. Only the goggles he'd been wearing at the time had saved his eyes. Everything else was cooked to a turn.

After seventy operations, the plastic surgeons had given up, assuring Samson that he was as pretty as he could ever expect to get. Which was really not pretty at all. The face they had managed to cobble together after such a marathon effort was ample proof that Nature still did such work far better than man.

His ears were stiff, shapeless stumps. The only hair on his head was what looked like a badly damaged caterpillar that had stiffened and died beneath the blunt, porcine snout that was his nose. The taut, lopsided opening of his mouth lacked lips. His fabricated eyelids didn't function very well. They opened and closed spastically in a manner that was unpleasant to observe.

The overall effect was of a man whose face had been removed, then disassembled, peeled, run over, and finally replaced in the dark by a drunk who was in a hurry.

"Is there some problem, Mark?" Samson inquired amiably.

"No. No. No problem. It's just been a punishing drive, is all. I'm having trouble getting the kinks out of my legs," Berghold said. He steeled himself to look at Samson's face without showing how it affected him.

Then he noticed what was wrong with the eyes. Not with the tortured, grafted tissue around them, but with the eyes themselves.

They were the worst eyes Mark Berghold had ever looked into. The irises were burgundy, the color of veinous blood. And there was nothing behind them. Nothing, at least, that a wise individual would want to get to know. They were windows on a frozen abyss. Berghold felt naked under their examination. He wanted to climb back in the Land Rover and jounce back the way they had come. Putting as much distance as possible between himself and those molesting eyes that had seized him and would not stray.

"Would you care for a *cerveza*? There is some that's been chilling inside on ice." Although his speech was impaired, Samson's words were clearly intelligible. Even through the impediment, his accent rang true. Berghold recalled that his dossier identified him as a native Bavarian.

"No. Thank you. I'm afraid I have only time enough to conduct our business before I must leave," Berghold replied. Then he recalled the rumors reported in the dossier about what happened to the doctors who failed to give Samson a human face. "I would accept your hospitality if I could. No offense is intended."

"Of course not," Samson said gently, "but you would be frank with me if my appearance sickened you, wouldn't you?" His face twisted in what might have been an effort at a smile. Samson enjoyed toying with the likes of Berghold and Sotus, bureaucrats who looked down on the killing fields from a lofty height and called themselves warriors.

Berghold was struggling to dredge up a suitable, diplomatic reply when Norman Sotus came to his rescue.

"You know you can depend on us, Samson, to be candid with you in all respects," Sotus interjected. He did his best to be as forceful as the situation required, but Samson's presence had a way of taking the starch out of most men's sails, Sotus being no exception.

"Who is it that you want me to kill, Mark?" Samson asked.

"John Paine," Berghold replied. "You might have heard of him."

"Who hasn't?" Samson said, adjusting the brim of his Panama hat with one small, blasted hand.

"He's gone bad. We think—" Berghold was cut off before he could elaborate further.

"I don't care what you think, Mark. Are you comfortable with two hundred fifty thousand as my reward for his disposal?" Samson asked.

Berghold found Samson's enormous fee almost as difficult to stomach as his face. It was simple extortion, and they both knew it. Something else they knew was that Berghold would not be there if he had any other option. Therefore, he would pay, regardless of how he felt about it.

"Yes" was all Berghold could manage as a response.

"Excellent. I will give you the number of an account at a bank in Lucerne. As soon as I have been informed that the money has been deposited, I will go to work. I will need all your data on Paine. You will provide me with a number from which I can acquire your most recent intelligence on his activities as I proceed. You will also provide me with a document signed by your Mr. Brock that grants me immunity from prosecution for any *violations* I might be obliged to commit during the mission. Agreed?" Samson said, with burgundy eyes boring into Berghold.

"Are you kidding?" It popped out before Berghold could prevent it. He was astounded. The bastard expected carte blanche for a one-man crime wave if he felt in the mood for it. They already had one of those on their hands. *That* was why they'd been forced to pursue the freak in the first place. They didn't need another, and from what Sotus had told him, Samson was just the gremlin to give them one that would be long remembered in the annals of law enforcement.

"Do I impress you as a man who jests with much regularity?" Samson inquired.

"No. But..." Berghold replied.

"I'm sure the Company can provide you with the kind of insulation you're looking for!" Sotus once again lunged into the gap that had just opened between his boss and the grotesque midget. As odious and troublesome and potentially embarrassing as such a free pass might be, Sotus knew Berghold would ultimately agree that they would be worse off if they did not concede to Samson's terms. "We also have an anonymous informant who's been feeding us regular information on Paine's whereabouts," Sotus added, hoping to keep the mercenary hooked.

"Really?" Samson said. "How fortunate for you. How unfortunate for Paine." He did not look away from Berghold as he spoke.

The two men stood there in silence for moments, staring at one another, with the warm sea's rhythmic pounding as background.

"Are you sure you won't have a cold beer?" Samson asked. "Now that our business is concluded."

Berghold remained transfixed by the bloody holes in the assassin's ruined face. What were they unleashing? Sotus had said that Samson was known for getting lost in his work. Everyone in the game knew what that meant. He wasn't a mechanic, an efficient technician who dealt in death. He was a serial killer who'd found a way to get paid for it. But now that he found himself in a position to dictate his terms, he wanted more than money. He wanted permission to do whatever he pleased in the pursuit of Paine. Even if it amounted to no more than psychopathic recreation. Looking at Samson, Berghold could easily envision what that might entail. Rape. Torture. Murder. Their dossier on Samson was replete with evidence that he had so indulged himself before. That was the reason the Company had avoided him for so long. Sotus had been right. Enlisting Samson to resolve their difficulty with John Paine was too much like sending a mad dog after a wolf.

"I think we should be going now, don't you, sir?" Sotus said.

It sounded like an excellent idea to Berghold. Of late, early retirement was sounding rather inspired, too. He had long operated on the assumption that his seniority with the Company would, over time, lead to ever more antiseptic and cerebral sorts of duties. Instead, the obverse had been true. His current predicament was a case in point. It seemed the more authority Berghold acquired, the deeper he had to sink his perfumed hands in the muck.

He knew it was all Paine's fault, but somehow he had the uneasy suspicion that it was larger and more menacing than that. Berghold's belly murmured to him that something greater than one man's fall from grace was required to compel a man of his stature to act as little more than a charmer of human snakes.

Berghold nodded his agreement to Sotus. His lieutenant had hit the mark squarely when he said there were few who were eager to meet Samson twice. What Samson amounted to as a man radiated from him like the dank, forbidding smell that met one at the mouth of some beast's lair. There was no limit to what he could do, or to his resulting glee as he did it.

Berghold wanted to get back to the plush hotel room and take a long shower. He needed some old scotch and a Latin lady of more recent vintage to help him erase the memory of the twisted little man before him.

Still he hesitated, wondering if there shouldn't be more to it than there had been.

"You needn't worry, Mark," Samson said cordially. "As long as I get what I want, you can trust that you will get what you want, as well. Soon we both will be satisfied."

That's what I'm afraid of, Berghold thought as he turned without another word and hurried with Sotus toward some more decent place.

10

A summer Saturday was well on its way by the time the woman awoke. It had been a strenuous and athletic, if deliciously rewarding, night for them both. Paine himself did not sleep as long. Still, when he silently left her bed, he felt more rested and calm than he had in many days. He found that to be a very good thing. It had been his primary goal when he called the brisk brunette the night before. He knew he could carry on indefinitely doing running battle with numerous opponents if he had to. He had done it before. But eventually it was necessary to recharge, lest he begin to lose the edge upon which his survival depended.

Constance Schwinn, unbeknownst to her, was helping Paine whet his edge. He found the double entendre that lurked within that metaphor amusing, and knew she would too if he shared it with her.

He was standing naked by the living room window watching the people in the park when he heard Schwinn slip out of bed. Her barefoot progress toward him was audible only because his hearing was acute and he was an inveterate listener. In the few hours they had been together, her innate quietness had become evident to him. Paine liked that. Loud people and places had been a problem for him ever since the war.

On such days Central Park presented a kaleidoscopic cross section of all the human elements of which the great metropolis was composed. The affluent and the homeless; the married and the single; conformists and bohemians; every color, every philosophy, every level and life-style imaginable. He could see them scattered over the Sheep Meadow in the sunshine beneath a sky nearly free of Manhattan's perennial shroud of haze. Under less perilous circumstances, Paine would have liked to go out with the woman and join them.

"Good morning," he said to her, letting her know he knew she had entered the room. He did not turn around when she came to him, slipped her arms around his waist, and flattened her nude front against his back.

"Did I tell you last night that you have fantastic buns?" she inquired, stroking the pelt on his hard belly affectionately with both hands.

"Repeatedly," Paine replied.

"Now you're supposed to tell me something complimentary, too," she said, running her nipples back and forth over him like infant fingertips.

"What would you suggest?" Paine said, smiling and chuckling softly as he felt his temperature beginning to rise.

"You could say I have the body of a high school cheerleader. I wouldn't mind that at all," she said.

"Neither would I," Paine replied. "If you *do*, would you mind letting me take a look at it?" he responded.

"You bastard! How morbid!" she wailed.

"I never promised you a healthy sense of humor," Paine said solemnly.

"You could tell me how saucy my breasts are. How high and firm and defiant," Constance cooed.

"It may come as no surprise to you that your boobs aren't the only organs that are high and firm and defiant in this room at the moment," Paine responded huskily.

"Are you suggesting that breakfast may not be the first item on the agenda this morning?" she giggled.

"No," he said, finally turning to face her, "what I'm doing is threatening you with a blunt instrument."

"My goodness!" she cried. "I guess you are!" She knew there was no denying the truth when the evidence was so readily at hand.

"Your goodness, Constance, has absolutely nothing to do with it," Paine said as he picked her up easily and headed back to the ring for a rematch.

They spent the remainder of the day indoors, enjoying one another's company in one way or another. As they talked, Paine explained to her how his troubles had been complicated from the start by having those who had been *for* him suddenly turn *against* him. He scrupulously maintained his cover story that he was a freelance journalist, and the woman assisted him in his effort by abstaining from asking any of the difficult questions that might have occurred to her.

Questions like: Why don't you go to the police? The FBI? The CIA? Interpol? Or any of the other watchdogs who would certainly be interested in a conspiracy involving homicidal, right-wing fanatics.

Constance Schwinn mainly listened and sympathized, sensing that that was really what he was seeking from her: not solutions so much as concern and compassion. She was thirty-six, old enough to know how to be energetically supportive while vertical, as well as while horizontal.

By the time night fell, Paine had grown weary of hiding out in the woman's home. He wanted to take her out like a normal man living a normal life; venture among the city's many attractions and have some fun. He knew it entailed a certain risk, but he was familiar with the precautions required to reduce that risk to an acceptable minimum.

Her prompting made the foray all the more attractive. Schwinn left the decision up to him as to whether they should go or stay; either way would lead to something entertaining, she was sure. But it would be a shame to settle for half a loaf, if they could seize the whole thing with a little extra effort.

That was an approach with which Paine wholeheartedly concurred.

Given the nature of her companion's attire Constance decided to dress down for the evening. She had fun with it, knowing there were few places as suited as Manhattan for adopting whichever image appealed to you most at a given time.

Moussing up her hair into what she thought of as a sweet-savage SoHo style, she slithered into a provocative pink tube top and painted-on jeans that left no doubt as to how hard she worked at staying in shape. High-heeled boots completed the creation of what Schwinn thought of as the "modern moll" look.

When Paine was slipping into his leather jacket as they prepared to leave, she said, "Don't you think you're overdressing, Neal? It's still eighty-something out there, you know."

"I have thin blood," Paine responded, smiling darkly and knowing the truth was exactly the reverse. He was a "clotter," an individual blessed by Nature with blood that was dense with the coagulant that rushed to close a wound as soon as it appeared. It was another one of the ways in which Paine was ideally suited to his trade. That particular attribute alone had saved his life numerous times.

He thought the minor lie preferable, however, to admitting to having both the Ingram machine-pistol and the Smith .357 concealed inside the lining of the jacket. He didn't think that knowledge would do much to enhance the quality of Constance Schwinn's evening. Then again, it might. She had been showing a marked inclination to taste deeply of the flavor of the "wild side" ever since their encounter on the plane. Paine had run across such women off and on throughout his career. They always intrigued him. Each possessed a very ordinary and civilized veneer that concealed a hellion who longed for a good chance to rebel. However, though they were basically alike, they differed widely when it came to how far they cared to venture on their safaris into anarchy.

Paine knew that often they themselves didn't know where to draw the line until they crossed it, and suddenly realized the fun had stopped, having been magically transformed to fear. Schwinn might find herself in that predicament if he told her he was heavily armed. So he opted for discretion instead.

They left her building separately, agreeing to rendezvous a few minutes later on Central Park South, in the best of cloak-and-dagger traditions. Though the woman took a businesslike approach to the procedure, Paine sensed she was having a good time. Schwinn exited by the front door; he once again used the service door in the rear.

Paine took a circuitous route on his way, tailing her for a few blocks to see if someone who was after him might have made the connection between the two of them despite his care. Schwinn had succeeded so well in adorning herself as a hot and fast item for their date that she was whistled at repeatedly from passing cars, as well as propositioned several times.

Some of the men might have mistaken her for one of the classy hookers who prowled the vicinity. The classy ones dressed within the limits of decency, unlike the girls who worked downtown in little more than their underwear, leaving small doubt as to what they offered besides a terrific view.

Unlike the numerous ladies of the night with whom she shared the busy streets, however, Constance responded to each loud and indecent proposal with a variety of gestures used locally to make clear she was neither interested nor pleased.

Once Paine was sure that they were alone, he re-joined her, and they set off in the general direction of Times Square.

"It's been a long time since I dressed like this for a date," she said, beaming up at him as she held his right arm captive in both of hers. "I'd forgotten how many horny characters are out looking for some action on a night like this. The last few blocks have been an education."

"I'll bet," he replied. He ran his eyes over her slowly with lusty appreciation. "You look good enough to eat."

"Back off, big boy, or we'll never make it to the movie," she said, laughing and thrusting herself against him pointedly.

"No offense, but they might have mistaken you for..." he attempted.

"...a *working girl*? Isn't that the polite way of saying it?"

"That's one of the polite ways," he answered.

"Do you really think that's possible?" she asked, looking herself over theatrically.

"Don't take it too hard. It's tough to make that call without a program these days. Has been for quite a while, come to think of it," Paine said.

"I'm *not* offended, Neal. At *my* age? Are you kidding? I'm overjoyed, to be honest." Listening to what she had just said, and knowing what she was about to say, Constance groaned, shook her head, rolled her eyes, and laughed. "God forbid my mother should hear this, but it's nice to know I could still sell it if I were so inclined!" She looked up into his eyes guiltily. "Is that an awful, degenerate thing to think? Does that mean I have a rotten self-image?"

"I seriously doubt it," he replied. "Considering all the trouble a lot of women go to to look like hookers, I'd say you've got plenty of company ... whether you're the picture of mental health or not."

"That's what I find so irresistible about you, baby, your warm, all-embracing cynicism," she said, grinning.

"Think nothing of it, Constance, but if *you're* old, what does that make me?" Paine glanced down at her obliquely from the corner of his eye, between scans of everyone and everything around them.

"Exceedingly well preserved, stud. *Exceedingly* well preserved!" She gave him a lewd look to go with the left-handed compliment, and gave his butt a solid squeeze to drive the point home.

"You're a long way from dry rot yourself," he said.

"I'm glad you noticed. I owe it all to Jane Fonda and vanity," she said.

"That sounds like a natural combo if I ever heard one," Paine responded bleakly.

They were approaching a local watering hole that looked only moderately popular, from the size of the crowd visible inside. It was the kind of place Paine favored.

"Care to sit and jaw for a spell before we hit the cinema?" he inquired.

"Precisely what I had in mind, as a matter of fact," she answered, steering him toward the entrance.

"You're using me, aren't you?" Schwinn said, after her rum collins and his Perrier had been served. The look on her face was out of synch with the question, as was the way she casually played with the plastic straw in her drink.

She appeared more curious than anything else.

When he failed to respond immediately, she continued, "Don't worry. I'm not upset. *Honestly*. I just like to be clear about what's going on in *things* like this."

Paine remained unsure of how best to answer her, and she seemed to be on a roll, so he was happy to let her do some more talking.

And Constance Schwinn was happy to talk.

"I know this little romance of ours, or mine, isn't going to last very long, and basically amounts to a case of the mutual hots, but it's something more practical for you than that, isn't it?" She stared at her ice cubes, thinking.

Paine thought he was starting to get the drift, and he admired her for being as quick to figure it out as she had been. Her mind was clearly as well maintained as her body.

When she looked up, her blue eyes joined with his.

"It's like a pit stop at the Indy Five Hundred,

I think. Or, what did they call those vacations the soldiers took during their time in Vietnam?" she asked quietly.

"R and R," Paine replied, "rest and recovery or recreation."

"Right. Rest and recreation. You saw me as a good way to regroup...relax...take on fuel ...out of the line of fire, right?" she asked.

"That's right. Have I been that obvious, or are you simply that sharp? If I've been obvious, you have my apology," he said with sincerity.

"There's no need to apologize...Neal." She gave the name a bit of extra emphasis. "You've been a real gentleman about the whole thing. Believe me, if you'd been a boor, I'd have noticed. I've had enough experience in identifying them." With that she gave him a relaxed and genuine smile.

"You really are quite a girl, Constance," Paine said, and meant it.

"Thanks, but I'm not a girl at all anymore, and you're not a boy. That's why we're being so grown-up about this. Ten years ago I might have been outraged, but I'm not so stuck on myself as I was back then. Not that I'll tolerate abuse, but you haven't been abusive. Quite to the contrary. You've been a wonder, both in the sack and out. And all the while you've been using me," she said.

"True," Paine said.

"But I've been using you, too," she said, then winked.

John Paine braced himself. Here it comes, he thought. She probably has a pistol pointed at my pecker even as we speak. Finally, the sparrow takes flight.

"I've been using you to inject some badly needed excitement into a life that had become long on obligations and terribly short on thrills. It felt like a prison of my own construction, and along you came to offer me escape. I appreciated that, and I knew it was unlikely to be offered free of charge. Hardly anything is," she said, lighting one of her infrequent cigarettes.

"True again," he said, and left it at that. The lady was doing just fine, in his opinion, all by herself.

"You're in even worse trouble than you've let on, aren't you?" she asked, changing the subject slightly.

"Yes. I am," he said.

"You aren't really a journalist, are you? You're something much darker and more deadly than that," she speculated. "I'd bet my life on it."

You already have, he thought, but said, "No. I really am a journalist, regardless of how nasty and sinister I might seem. If I were the character you suspect me to be, I'd hardly be taking cover under an unsuspecting woman's skirts, regardless of how delightful the view might be under there." Paine paused to give her time to absorb the compliment and smile. "I'd be out laying waste to my enemies, the way a macho menace should."

As lies went, Paine considered that one to be at least par for the course.

Constance blew smoke and took a sip of her drink before she gently shook her head, and said, "In my heart I know that to be cow flop of the purest kind. Fortunately, I don't much care. Whatever the truth may be, you make me feel like I've been too damn careful about a lot of things for too damn long. I think taking chances just might be a better way of life."

"Don't bet on it," Paine said.

"Tell me one thing truthfully. Even if all the rest is fiction," she implored.

"Sure thing," Paine said.

"Is Neal Heck your real name?" she asked.

"The truth?" A large question mark took shape on his strong features.

"The *truth*," Schwinn stressed.

"No. It's not," he admitted reluctantly.

"Ha! I knew it," she exclaimed.

"You must promise not to share this with anyone," he said soberly.

"I swear," she replied with lips pursing slightly.

"It's Buford," he whispered.

"Buford!" she cried.

"Shhhh! You promised, remember?" he said with a hint of desperation.

"Neal Buford?" she whispered, leaning toward him intently.

"Buford Neal Heck," he said, shaking his head.

"You shouldn't be so defensive about it. It has a nice, strong ring to it. A little aristocratic even," she glowed, covering one of his hands with both of her own.

"It does?" he responded doubtfully.

"Sure. I can see why your mother chose it. It

suits you; nice, strong, and honorable," Constance said.

"Well, *strong*, at least," he said.

The movie they went to after they left the bar was pure escapist fare: romance, revenge, murder, and mayhem; the bad guys died because the good guy killed them. It wasn't the way things really worked, and for that, John Paine was heartily thankful. He liked keeping the way things really worked on the sidewalk outside the theater. He would have enjoyed it even without a title that struck a sympathetic chord. Because the story on the screen was the way it would be if John Paine had his way. The title was simply gravy, *Hard to Kill*.

For him, it might serve as a fitting epitaph.

Surveying the sea of strange faces in the darkness of the auditorium around them, he hoped he wouldn't be needing one in the near future.

11

They returned to Schwinn's apartment the way they had left it, splitting up a few blocks away in order to enter the building separately. Again, Paine's reconnaissance discovered nothing that seemed to be amiss. The woman was standing by her front door, waiting for him patiently, when he arrived.

"No trouble?" she asked, looking up at him as she worked her key into the lock.

"None that I noticed," he responded.

"Good. The night's still young," she said, opening the door, "and I don't want any interruptions in what I have planned for you." Constance tossed a playful look over her shoulder as they entered.

"So much for the *rest* part of this R and R, right?" Paine returned amiably.

"You got it, soldier."

With the door closed and bolted, she pressed herself against him, wrapping her slender arms around his lean waist.

"Why don't you pour us a little brandy while

I make myself more comfortable? You know where it is," she said.

"Are the drinks to be served in the arena, ma'am? Or will her ladyship be returning for some preliminary flaunting before the main event?" Paine asked, smiling down at her pale, appealing face.

"Hmmm," she murmured, scowling prettily as if the question presented her with a difficult decision. "I don't want to rush into anything," she said tentatively.

"That makes one of us," Paine said, sliding his hands under the stretchy fabric of her tube top to caress the smooth warmth of her back.

"Stop that, you animal," she objected, but not at all convincingly. "I shall return," she assured him, backing away. "I have a few recently purchased items I'd like to model for you. I've been saving them for a very special occasion. Heaven knows they're not appropriate for anything else!"

With that, Constance flounced off toward the bedroom, leaving Paine to attend to the refreshments.

The tall walnut liquor cabinet in a corner of the living room was well stocked with the best of everything, like the rest of the place, where original prints and paintings occupied most of the walls. An inked sketch that hung inside its frame only a few feet away had "Picasso" scrawled in the lower right-hand corner. Paine took his time with the preparations. He didn't consider himself an expert on women, but didn't think it took one to know the lady would require a few minutes to accomplish her transformation.

He selected two delicate rose crystal snifters, and splashed enough brandy into each to cover the bottom. From the bedroom came a sound that was nearly a squeak. He paused when he heard it, listening closely, curious. It might have been a squeal of delight from a woman posing before a mirror, wearing something lewd enough to spread embarrassment through a bordello.

Paine knew the less inhibited sorts like Schwinn could be relied on to make some strange sounds on occasion, usually when a man least expected it. It was part of their charm, though he sometimes found it unsettling.

When no further such sounds disturbed the silence, he carried the drinks to the long couch across from the love seat and set them on the coffee table. Paine settled onto the couch, raised a snifter to his lips, savored the ferocious fumes, and returned it to its place beside its mate.

He relaxed himself, taking one deep breath after another. As minute after minute passed, he was increasingly less pleased with himself for not having checked out every room immediately upon their return. It was sloppy procedure. He hadn't even left a telltale on the door to signal an intrusion: something like a tiny scrap of paper wedged between the door and its frame at the top above the hinge that would dislodge if the door was opened. Or a strategically placed sugar cube beneath the throw rug in the entry that would crush beneath the weight of an intruder's foot.

He damned his own negligence as Schwinn's absence and the unnatural silence that attended it went on far too long. He'd taken the "R and R" thing too seriously, allowing himself to forget momentarily that he was in the midst of a war. The old fear rose up within him, whispering that he was about to pay dearly for his lapse; that the woman might already have paid for it... in full.

Maybe it's nothing, he told himself. Maybe she's pondering which perfume to apply.

He hoped that was the way it was. If so, what he was about to do would cause no harm. It would amount to nothing worse than overcaution, and in Paine's chosen field, overcaution was not a vice. If it went the other way, he might still, with luck and skill, be able to save her life.

He did the rest of it by the numbers then, silently rising; balancing his bulk on the balls of his feet; gliding to the jacket where he'd left it by the door; removing the Smith .357 and automatically inspecting its loads; extinguishing all the lights, starting with the one farthest from the bedroom first.

The bedroom light itself had also been switched off. Thus, when the last lamp on his way to it died, the apartment was plunged into almost total darkness. Only the vague city glow from the windows prevented the pervasive gloom from being complete.

Paine took care to not look toward the windows as he let his irises expand. His night vision was excellent. Steadily the black wall before him shaded into gray, and he could see. Not well, but he could see.

He crept down the hall soundlessly toward the onyx rectangle that was the entrance to the bedroom, with the Smith cocked and held ready at port arms. There was no longer any question as to the intruder's presence. The only questions remaining were who it was, whether he had disposed of Constance yet, and how he intended to kill Paine. He knew that none of his pursuers had anything in mind for him that was less than terminal.

He flattened himself against the wall, edging inch by inch closer to the opening, feeling the adrenaline leaking into his bloodstream, making him sweat and speeding his heart, turning up the pressure to prepare him.

He waited, hoping for some break in the perfect silence that would tell him it was time to move.

When none came, he launched his big body through the doorway, extending the gun with both hands, throwing himself to his left as he aimed at the dark form on the bed...

and squeezed.

"It's about time, darling! I was beginning to think you'd fallen asleep out there!" Constance chuckled at him from the lagoon of shadow in which she lay.

Paine raised the muzzle and removed his finger from the trigger in one single, sudden motion.

He stood there in a crouch, trembling, breathing hard, feeling the usual combat chill rush through him. "Jesus!" was all he could manage as she flicked the light on next to the bed.

"Dashing as usual, I—" Schwinn went quiet

abruptly when she saw the masterpiece of blued steel in his hands.

"That's a good way to get yourself killed, sweetheart," he said when he had the air to spare.

Paine registered in the back of his mind the wisps of crimson satin she had donned to please him, but his body was in the wrong mode to do more than simply note their presence.

"I'm sorry, Neal. I just changed my mind. I thought I'd surprise you by being quiet as a mouse and seeing how long it took for you to get tired of waiting for me to show up," she said. Her expression was one of sincere contrition. Her blue eyes danced back and forth from his face to the gun.

"Women!" It was almost a snarl as he wheeled about and stalked back through the doorway into the hall.

Paine did not hear the closet door across from the bed open behind him as he left the room.

But he heard Schwinn's terrified shriek.

It left no room for doubt about the reality of the danger this time.

Paine was fast for his size. He was back in the doorway with the gun grasped tightly, held at shoulder level, in both hands in a matter of seconds.

But Martina Vlota was a jungle cat.

With all her lithe strength and speed, she snatched Schwinn off the bed, and was holding her by the hair from behind as a shield when Paine reappeared.

The two women were close to one another in build. Close enough to provide Paine with next to nothing at which to shoot. The only portions of Vlota that he could see clearly were an occasional glimpse of one eye and the hand that held the muzzle of the nine-millimeter Heckler & Koch pressed firmly against Schwinn's skull directly behind the ear.

"It's a night for surprises, isn't it, Paine?" Vlota said in her eerie, androgynous voice.

Paine found himself staring into his lover's fear-crazed eyes as he directed the snout of the Smith at the sweet depression at the base of her throat.

"Remember me, Paine? The girl you left behind?"

That this was the one who had been his constant shadow for so long, he was sure. But all the rest remained a perfect blank.

"Drop the gun, Paine, or I'll serve this bitch to you en brochette!" Vlota snapped.

"Go right ahead," Paine replied flatly. "She's nothing to me."

"Neal!" Constance cried out to him with desperate disbelief, receiving a vicious yank on her hair by Vlota as her reward.

"But she's the only thing keeping you alive at the moment, so you might want to think it over before you waste her," Paine said.

Paine wasn't sure of too much at that instant, but he knew that he meant what he said. There was no way he was putting the gun down. To do so would do neither himself nor the woman any good. At best, it would only delay what the intruder had planned for both of them. As it stood, both Schwinn and his nemesis were likely to die, and do so almost simultaneously, in the next few minutes. But that would leave John Paine alive, and as regrettable as that outcome might be, he knew he could find a way to live with it.

"You don't think I mean it, do you?" Vlota snarled. "You still underestimate me!"

"Who's underestimating who?" Paine inquired. "I don't think you're bluffing. I think you're going to kill her. And I'm not bluffing, either. The moment you pull the trigger, and blow her brains all over the room, I'm going to empty this Smith through her warm body into yours. It'll be one hell of a mess, but guess who'll do the walking away?" His stance never wavered as he spoke. Both he and Vlota knew the .357 could do that and more. Schwinn's flesh would be about as helpful as screaming obscenities at a speeding train.

"Don't you want to say good-bye to your woman before I put a slug through her head?" Vlota asked tauntingly.

"I don't think you have the picture, whoever you are," Paine spat back. "She's not my *woman*. She's just a piece of ass. That's why I won't lose any sleep over what happens to her. But I'm a decent guy, so sure, 'Good-bye, Constance. It's been keen.' So what's next? Do we start shooting now?"

Vlota didn't respond immediately. Her plan was not working. Paine was supposed to plead with her for the woman's life at the very least. She wanted to hurt him as badly as she could, and didn't mind dying in the process so long as she went to her grave knowing she had gotten it done. Discovering his involvement with the woman had seemed the perfect opportunity to do him harm, but it was worthless if he didn't care.

And Vlota was becoming more convinced by the moment that Paine's arctic indifference was no act. If that was true, then all she had accomplished was risking her own life by underestimating him *again*. Was it possible some men had no feelings at all? The man aiming the gun at her hostage seemed to be living proof that it was.

"Maybe I'll shoot *you* instead, and let you kill her when you fire at me!" Vlota ventured.

"That won't work," Paine replied simply.

"Really?" Vlota's English was excellent, but it bore the unmistakable tinge of her native tongue. Paine kept trying without success to identify it.

"Really," Paine replied. "If you so much as twitch that piece in my direction, I'll open fire. And yes, Constance will die. So will you. But I won't. It always gets back to the bottom line, doesn't it? By the way, who the hell are you, and why have you been dogging me?"

"Don't pretend you don't remember me. Even *your* victims are not so numerous that you should lose track," Vlota said.

"Why don't you let me see you better? Quit being so shy," Paine suggested with a grim smile.

"I think not. Perhaps if I refresh your memory, it will all come back to you," Vlota responded.

"Are you an operative? Is that it?" Paine asked.

The question seemed to incense the woman beyond words. For moments she could manage no more than enraged, inarticulate sounds. "What else would I be, you bastard? Who else could follow you halfway around the world? And without your knowing it!"

"I won't deny you that," Paine agreed, "but if you're a player, then what is this all about? Something I did to you?"

"Yes! Yes! Yes!" Vlota hissed.

"Don't you think you're taking it kind of hard, whatever it was? If it was in the line of business, it was nothing personal. You must know that. I'd say you've gotten carried away with this whole thing." Paine was becoming genuinely confused. There was no such thing as vendettas between people in the game based on any damage that was done during a mission. Everyone knew that. It seemed, however, that his nemesis found this to be a tradition she preferred to disregard. At least where he was concerned.

Who is she? Paine asked himself.

The girl you left behind, she had said.

He sent a part of his mind that he could spare racing back through his memories, searching for the incident in which he had sinned against her so grievously. But the information he had was insufficient. Black hair, cut in a stylish mid length that was neither masculine nor feminine. Swarthy skin. Lean. Slightly above average in height for a woman. Apparently adept at the rough stuff, despite her severe miscalculation of his feelings for Constance Schwinn.

The woman's hasty assumption of a deep emotional involvement between them was, in fact, so contrary to the behavior of agents in general, and Paine himself in particular, that it amounted to little more than wishful thinking. The woman *wanted* them to be in love because that would fit into her design for retribution quite neatly. The gap between what she wanted and the way it really was had been easily bridged by the span of her imagination.

That was what happened when an agent let her feelings take precedence over cold-blooded reason. *That* was the rationale behind not taking anything personally in the business. There was nothing noble and idealistic about it. You simply lost the ability to think clearly the moment passion took over. And, quite often, you were forcefully "retired" shortly thereafter. By someone with a much cooler head.

It was axiomatic in the game that sleeping with someone (be they players or be they not) amounted to nothing more than attending to an innate and inescapable biologic need. There might be more to it than that, but usually there wasn't. Espionage as a profession and romantic sexuality were almost perfectly incompatible. The former was founded on deceit, distrust, betrayal, and a cynical contempt for all genuine feelings, characteristics that were as surely ruinous to the latter as a generous sprinkling of salt to a slug.

Every operative knew there was no requisite link between what went on *in* bed, regardless of how torrid the coupling might have been, and what took place *out* of it. Copulating with someone didn't mean losing one's heart. All that was lost was a few milliliters of body fluid. It did not amount to much in the way of a bond; hardly enough to risk dying for.

Paine's intercourse with Schwinn, as intensely satisfying as it had been, entailed no more emotional bonding than he felt for a good steak at the end of a meal. His nemesis must have known that. That she had chosen to ignore something so elementary did not bode well for her continued good health.

"Maybe you would feel differently if *you* had been the one who went for the long swim instead of *me!*" With their lethal standoff appearing to have reached a delicate balance of sorts, Vlota relaxed slightly. She released her grip on Schwinn's hair, and began to caress her teasingly while the other hand kept the H & K nine-millimeter tucked snugly behind her ear. "You called him Neal. Which means you do not know who and what he really is," Vlota said to Schwinn. "Would you like me to tell you the kind of monster you've been dropping your pants for?"

"Yes!" Constance whispered, but only because she believed it was the answer the crazy woman wanted.

"I think I will rape this pretty baby of yours instead of kill her. That will be more like what you did to me, Paine," Vlota said. With one hand she started to slowly and sensually remove Schwinn's bra.

"No! Please don't!" Schwinn pleaded. Fear and revulsion competed for dominion inside her as the killer's cool, dry hands glided over her in a knowing and intimate fashion.

"I still don't know what you're talking about,"

Paine replied, "but if it makes you feel better to rape her, go right ahead. She'll find it a lot easier to recover from than death. If you're doing it for my benefit, though, you might as well skip it. I'm not into that kinky routine. It does nothing for me at all." True as that was, Paine was worldly enough to tell that it did quite a bit for his nemesis.

That was when it came to him.

Middle-European accent. A switch-hitting sparrow, turned assassin. A lesbian androgyne who could pass as easily for male as for female. A good agent, but sadistic and egocentric.

And "the long swim." That was why her name had never occurred to Paine. Not in all the ruminations over who his nemesis might be. He'd cashed her out; sent her to "the deep six." She was supposed to have been divided up by sharks long before.

Thus, whatever the woman's shortcomings might be, she had manifested a talent that would take her far...

Especially if she could teach others how to do what she had done ... for whatever price she cared to name.

She had risen from the dead.

Which qualified her to start her own religion if John Paine wasn't mistaken.

"Martina Vlota," he stated simply. "You're a lot harder to kill than I took you for after that dumb move you pulled."

Vlota's response to the combined recognition and slander was twofold: first, she sunk her hard fingers into Schwinn's naked breast, squeezing it viciously, making the woman scream, doing her best to injure the true object of her hatred by proxy if she could; second, she hurled a long, scalding stream of expletives at Paine, none of which moved him in the least, his grasp of Albanian being as limited as it was.

"Dumb move!" Vlota snapped. "I had you completely fooled! I shot you!" The slice of her face that was revealed behind Schwinn's head was a taut rictus of boiling spleen. Paine was glad Constance couldn't see it. It would have been sufficient to make her panic, and any false move on anyone's part at the moment would force him to use the Smith.

"Those weren't the moves I had in mind," Paine said. It was the Albanian's attempt at the coup de grace that had gotten her all wet. They both knew that.

"You want to see a dumb move? I'll show you a dumb move!" She spit the words at Paine like a cobra as her dark hand tightened around the small automatic.

This is what happens when you don't do the job right. Your victims come back to haunt you. Paine lashed himself as he waited for Vlota to pull the trigger.

Though his eyes were on the two women, what he saw was a moonless night in the midst of the Adriatic.

It was all coming back to him.

Including a few dumb moves of his own that had nearly gotten him killed.

12

The assignment had looked like a walk in the park when he received it. He was to baby-sit an Albanian defector until the desk jockeys decided what to do with him. The two of them booked passage together on an Italian vessel, a floating luxury resort, that would take them from Naples for a long, sunbaked excursion through the Adriatic.

It was understood that some of the defector's fellow countrymen would take his decision to change sides very hard since the man knew many things they would much prefer keeping to themselves. Which meant their security service would be under orders to find and silence him before he could sing all the verses of that forbidden song.

Had the man been from some other country, that state of affairs might have been cause for serious concern, and the resulting precautions that went with it. But everyone in the game knew the Albanians were a greater threat to each other when they got excited than they were to anyone else. Their collective ineptitude was equaled only by their indifference to decorum and the gratuitous malice they traditionally displayed in all things.

No one had much in the way of respect or affection for them, least of all John Paine. Nonetheless, he'd prepped himself for the job by reviewing the current files on all the hitters they were likely to send against him. Including that of Martina Vlota. But it had been a halfhearted effort. For which he had very nearly paid with his life.

Paine had committed what he knew to be the mortal sin of underestimating his opponent. In later days, with the mission successfully completed, his debriefers acknowledged it to be a hard sin to avoid when your opponent was Albania.

He remained watchful for the first few days after they left port, scrutinizing everyone else on board in search of one of the individuals described in the files. However, once he had assured himself that the boat was clean, he lowered his guard. That was what Martina Vlota had been waiting for, and she took full advantage of it when it came.

She was masquerading as a steward. That was why Paine had missed her. In his mind, Vlota was categorized as "female." Thus, he never thought to look for her among the male passengers or members of the crew. Sexual chameleons were as rare in the game as they were in society in general. Their bizarre ability to switch back and forth between apparent genders at will gave them a distinct advantage over everyone when the need for camouflage arose.

Vlota knew this. It was her secret weapon. Though she took great pride in it, there were few who knew of it, even among her Albanian colleagues. That was why there was no mention of the trait in her file. Vlota understood that the more occult her skill remained, the more deadly it would be. She also knew that the strange quality with which fate had blessed her was likely to get her shunned even by her comrades should it become common knowledge.

It was one thing to be bisexual in the amoral world she inhabited. Such a capacity to adapt was required of women like herself who had started out in the trade as little more than sexual tools. But it was always assumed that even ravens and sparrows were more or less "natural" underneath. They simply worked both sides of the street because it was required of them.

Such, however, had never been the case with Martina Vlota. She had always been a perfect misfit when it came to sexual orientation. Anatomically she was a complete female, albeit one who was built along spare and rather boyish lines: narrow hips, wide shoulders, small breasts that were easily concealed, a ropily muscled physique, and a voice that was neither masculine nor feminine.

Psychologically she was comparably complete as a male. It was the ultimate mismatch of body and mind. Vlota thought of herself as a man perversely forced to inhabit a woman's form. It was her sincere male self-image more than her build that made her so convincing in her impersonation of a man. In truth, the male was the easier gender for her to portray. When she became a woman, Vlota had to work at it, paying conscious attention to facial expressions, gestures, and body language that had always been foreign to her vision of herself.

Vlota's sexual desires revolved exclusively around women, and she considered herself heterosexual. She had had sex with men many times in the line of work, but never without the need to overcome her distaste at indulging in what she knew to be a homosexual perversion. Similarly, whenever a mission required her to parade her lithe body in a bikini at the beach, she found the lusty looks of men a constant source of both embarrassment and irritation.

Thus, Vlota had slipped into the role of steward on the vessel with instinctive ease. The subservient part of it was an effort since she was not only a man inside, but a proud and aggressive one, as well. She lived as the "husband" to a voluptuous blonde who fully understood who wore the pants in their relationship and who did the serving around their home. But Vlota knew how to mask her personality as well as her sex.

Therefore, by the end of the first week of the cruise, Vlota basked in the assurance that the brawny, cruel-looking American agent had been successfully deceived. His cold eyes had passed over her several times without so much as a tremor of recognition. She was nothing more than another miscellaneous element in the mobile human landscape that was the ship's population. That was the way Vlota liked it. Let Paine focus his attention on the herd of eager, skimpily clad beauties that crowded all the decks constantly. As Vlota served them, and flirted, and enjoyed the view.

When she decided she had waited long enough, Vlota went for Paine. He had to be eliminated first, while the element of surprise still gave her the advantage, before she moved on to the traitor and what he deserved.

Her opportunity came late one night when most of the ship was asleep. Paine left the cabin he shared with the defector to take a stroll on deck, smoke a cigarette, and savor the moonless expanse of the rolling sea that surrounded them. In retrospect, Vlota realized that the sport coat he wore should have told her something at the time. Paine wasn't the sort to dress up for much of anything, least of all a midnight ramble by himself beneath the sparkling stars.

But she knew the chances to take him unobserved were likely to be few and far between, and the days remaining on the voyage were rapidly dwindling. That made her eager. Too eager. And she was totally convinced that his guard was down, leaving him wide open. She was confident that she had duped the notorious CIA enforcer. Too confident.

Martina Vlota...the plain, friendless slum child whose first decent job was turning tricks on command for the government...had used her twisted nature and taste for bloodshed to rise through the ranks of agents to the violent heights occupied by predators of the stature of John Paine.

It was no mean achievement.

She was, perhaps, intoxicated by it.

Making no effort to conceal her approach, Vlota had strolled to within ten feet of Paine's broad back, removing the silenced .223 Baretta automatic from her starched linen jacket as she drew near. Then, as he relaxed against the rail, she had taken one last rapid glance in both directions along the deck to make sure they were alone, before opening fire in midstride.

Six times she squeezed the trigger in half as many seconds, shredding the sport coat in a tight little grouping over the heart. She'd expected Paine to tumble overboard from the savage impact of the cluster of small, but high-velocity, bullets. Instead of falling forward, however, he had staggered back away from the rail, groaning and twisting like a man in torment, before slumping to the deck on his back.

During the terrible hours that followed, Martina Vlota told herself a thousand times... *that* was when she should have fired the insurance shot into Paine's head. Without moving a single step closer. There was no good reason to move in as she had.

There *was* a bad reason, however. She relished wetwork. She delighted in delivering the coup de grace up close. Delighted in the effect of muzzle blast at point-blank range. It was her taste for gore that prodded her forward, and was her undoing.

Paine lay there with his mouth hanging open, staring like the newly dead at the galactic canopy that domed the sea. He gave the swarthy steward with the dangling gun his very best corpse impersonation. He'd seen enough of them to deliver a convincing performance. Looking dead, however, had not been the problem. It was the acute pain caused by the slugs smashing into the Kevlar that had been the real challenge at the time.

The instant he was hit, Paine had known his only chance lay in making clear to the shooter that, dead or not, he was no more threat. Though he had been cautious enough to don the Second Chance vest before he left the cabin, he hadn't been sufficiently concerned to bring his gun. Therefore, he had to decoy the killer close enough for his hands and feet to be brought to bear.

Which meant getting silent and still and staying that way so his attacker didn't decide to play it safe and lob a few more rounds at him from a distance; rounds that were likely to be aimed at some of the vast territory the Kevlar didn't protect.

It took all his self-control to squelch his body's screaming need to react to the molten spikes that had just been pounded into his back. But he was able to manage it by steeling himself, aided by the certainty that he would die if he did not.

The steward had only paused briefly after Paine's bulk hit the deck before advancing. It had, however, seemed a good deal longer than that as Paine lay there waiting for the final bullet to smash through his skull. Naked, vulnerable, exposed. Fighting the instinct to do something, *anything*, to defend himself was nearly as hellish as stifling the pain.

But then his assailant came to him, crouching

next to his still form, savoring the joy of the kill as the weapon lifted slowly...

until Paine released all his pent-up fury in a sudden explosion of strength and swift, conditioned agility...

sweeping the weapon aside with one hand,

seizing the starched jacket front with the other,

drawing his knees up tight against his chest, and

driving both feet into the steward's midsection,

thrusting savagely, lifting his attacker like a thing made of rags off the deck and up into the air,

as the silencer spit and spit again; the bullets whining down the length of the ship to ricochet out into the night,

letting go his grip as the assassin clawed desperately to seize the rail and Paine's powerful thighs catapulted that light, supple body out over it...

to plunge silently down into the salty embrace of the featureless rolling swells.

The sound of Vlota's impact with the waves was absorbed by the distant thunder of the vessel's churning wake.

The ordeal was over then for Paine, who remained there sprawled next to the rail for a while, waiting for the agony and the killing frenzy to subside; indifferent to his attacker's fate; content in the assurance it would not be one that he would care to share.

But for Martina Vlota, the ordeal had only

just begun. Paine's ploy had foxed her completely. He had gone off like a bomb at her feet, launching her over the side before she'd even had the time to be afraid. Then, unbelievably, she was falling through the warm night air and smashing headfirst into the endless wilderness of water far below.

The shock of her brutal immersion in the tepid sea left her disoriented for seconds until she heard and felt the ominous boom of the ship's huge screws approaching. Then her lifelong instincts as a survivor took over, and she struck out with a powerful overhand stroke, sprinting at a right angle to the vessel's course, putting precious yards between herself and the whirling propeller blades.

When they were safely past, and the gaily lighted silhouette of the liner grew steadily smaller, leaving her behind, Martina Vlota felt a fear begin to rise in her such as nothing she had ever known.

The ship was all there was.

And the American bastard had thrown her overboard.

In the middle of the night.

To drown. By herself. All alone.

She desperately considered swimming after the ship as it continued to shrink and the abyssal darkness it had interrupted settled over her and spread like vast black wings. She'd even started after it when the absurdity, the childishness, of the notion occurred to her. *Dolphins* were equipped for such feats; humans weren't. Even if she *could* catch up to it, what would she have accomplished? There was only one passenger who knew she was gone, and he wasn't likely to be alerting the captain. She would have had to parallel the ship for hours until the morning was far enough advanced for the passengers to come on deck.

That was all the stuff of demented fantasies.

Which left the possibility of swimming to the nearest shore. How far was that? Vlota asked herself. About fifty miles at the very least, was her best estimate.

Fifty ... miles.

What was the farthest she had ever swum? A quarter mile, perhaps, when she was feeling energetic.

Which direction should she take?

How deep was the water beneath her feet? A thousand feet? Ten thousand?

How long would it take for the sharks to arrive?

Vlota strained to keep the lights of the ship in sight as long as she possibly could, lifting her head when she rose to the crest of a wave to catch one more feverish glimpse, until they were finally and irretrievably gone.

Then she had the Adriatic to herself.

And the Adriatic, in its turn, had her.

There was no measuring the passage of time as Vlota steadily trod the fine, undulating line between the sparkling infinity above and the obsidian beckoning void below. It may have been several hours, but the darkness still held fast when she realized that she must surely die and only a coward would prolong the agony of fending off the inevitable for too long.

Better to surrender; dive down; breathe deep; and be done with it.

While John Paine carved another notch in his gun and lived on. Laughing through the rest of his many days at how easily he had played her for a fool. Sharing the story of the way he had done it with other ruthless devils like himself. Chuckling over how it must have been for Vlota in the end; how long and hopeless and slow. Making bets over how long it had taken her to realize that she was no match for the sea; to concede defeat; and let it claim her as another prize.

When she screamed, seabirds flushed into flight from their floating perches nearby. The single note she roared went on and on, fueled by a rage that was greater even than her despair. The note was a word, and the word was "No!"

She would not panic. She would not waste her strength swimming stupidly in circles and going no place at all. She recalled mentions in conversations overheard among other members of the crew that they traveled in a shipping lane. Such lanes were invisible highways across the sea. All she had to do was remain where she was, a traveler stranded by the side of the road. Another ship would come along before too long. She would attract their attention somehow, and they would rescue her.

That was the way it would be. Vlota declared it, as if the declaration would be enough to make it so. And she vowed, once her salvation was accomplished, there would be only one purpose serving as foundation for her future.

To avenge herself on John Paine.

To lay waste to his life, and teach him torment, the way he had taught it to her.

To kill his family... his friends... his associates... his *life*. Until he dwelt in the midst of a void as empty and forbidding as the sea itself. With no shore in sight; nothing solid to which he might cling; surrounded by merciless appetites; and feeling like a simple fool.

Vlota was ready for the first taste of an everlasting feast of revenge.

All she needed was a ride.

But no ship came her way. Not until the sun was well past its zenith, and she had been in the water something like twelve hours. When one finally did, a tanker, she could tell, from its low-slung configuration, it was a mile away and moving fast. By then Martina Vlota was too exhausted, scorched, and waterlogged to do anything but curse and cry.

Had she drifted out of the lane? Should she try to swim to the place the tanker had been? Were the shipping lanes really like highways, only a few yards wide? Or were they broad belts equal to a hundred roads on land, as she assumed? What if she swam for hours to reposition herself, only to have the next ship appear in the place where she had been before? Would she lose her mind, her will to live, if that happened?

Vlota was unwilling to take that chance. Even with her longing for retribution to fuel her, it took everything she had to stay afloat, fighting the urge to sleep, which became greater and more irresistible with each hour that passed. If she fell asleep, she would die. Only the constant motion of her limbs kept her face above the perpetual procession of waves that rocked her in a liquid cradle until...

she awoke to the fearful darkness of another night, not knowing how long she had slept, or how she could have slept and lived. With the overpowering craving for sleep reduced, she realized that she was racked with thirst. Again, she knew, to drink of the tangy salt water would mean certain death for her. As fragile as her grasp on life had become, stomach cramps alone would be enough to break that tenuous grip.

Vlota would never be able to recall when the hallucinations started: the voices calling to her, the vessels that suddenly appeared very near with raucous music playing from their decks, the people who would pause while they were swimming by to wave and smile. She could not even say with certainty that all of it had been the fantasies of a failing mind. She doubted the circling dorsal fins and occasional nibbles at her legs had been such, at the very least.

By the time the tramp steamer spotted her the next morning, Martina Vlota had been treading water for thirty hours and was more dead than alive. It was two days before she came around enough to realize she had been saved. In the meantime she had wailed and carried on like a mad thing in her sleep.

The only English-speaking member of the crew took note of a word she kept repeating. It saddened him to hear it. When he told his shipmates what she said, they, too, were moved. They had no trouble imagining the kind of ordeal it must have been for her. Being swept overboard was one of the great fears they all shared. They assumed that, somehow, that was the misfortune that had befallen her.

Small wonder that she should speak of suffering in her sleep. More than speak, *rail* against it, chant a single word like a damning curse over and over, as if the sea had stolen everything from her mind but that thought. It seemed to occupy every cell of her brain.

As the sailors listened, Vlota whispered it, whined it, snarled it, chuckled it. Voiced it in a thousand different ways.

"Paine!"

"Paine!"

"Paine!"

Her saviors were correct in their interpretation, if only inadvertently.

"Paine" was all she thought, and "Paine" to her meant suffering.

13

"She's not the one you want, Vlota. I'm the one you want," John Paine ventured.

If it was possible to end their standoff without bloodshed, that was the way he wanted it to be. As badly as he yearned to finish the job he'd started when the Albanian tried to kill him on the boat, Paine balked at bathing in the blood of Constance Schwinn. She wasn't a player. She was a civilian. His personal code of ethics demanded that he risk *his* life, if necessary, to try to avoid taking *hers*.

If Vlota left him no choice, he would kill them both; with regret regarding Schwinn and relish toward the murderer of Father Beck and Bill Mitchell, and the architect of his false image as a homicidal maniac. He preferred, however, to settle it with her more cleanly than that.

"That's right," Vlota spat back, "you're the one I want, and you're the one I will have."

"I have my serious doubts about that," Paine responded, "but who knows? Maybe you've improved with age and experience. The way it stands, though, we're never going to find out, are we?" Paine relaxed his stance slightly, seeking to defuse the situation with his posture as well as his words.

Vlota answered him with silence. Paine knew that she knew she had committed another fatal error of judgment, like the one on the boat, by miscalculating the value of her hostage. He knew, too, that she was too arrogant to gracefully acknowledge her error as most agents would have done in her situation. Nonetheless, he believed she would take her life and leave with it if he handed it to her. Without so much as a fragment of finesse, more than likely, but Paine knew better than to sweat fine points of style when dealing with an Albanian.

As the deadly duel continued, Constance Schwinn pretended that she wasn't there at all. It had the distinct feel of a nightmare, and everyone knew even the worst of nightmares eventually came to an end when you awoke to discover it was only something you ate. Or some*one*, she goaded herself, in this particular case. The nine-millimeter muzzle pressed to her skull had gone far to turn her into a comely alabaster mannequin clad now only in matching garter belt, bikinis, and whorehouse hose.

"I'll make you a deal," Paine continued. "We'll call this one a draw. You don't kill her. I don't kill you. We break clean, and schedule a rematch at some later date and some other place, preferably where there's no bystanders to get in our way. What do you say?"

"You take me for a fool if you think I will fall for something so obvious!" Vlota said frigidly.

Paine took a deep breath to calm his annoyance before he replied. A total lack of common sense was another attribute for which Albanian operatives were renowned.

"I don't expect you to take my word for anything, Vlota. The three of us will simply move this little tableau of ours, with the greatest of care, from here to the front door. Where you will make your exit. You and I both know exactly what will happen if either of us decides to try something cute before we disengage, don't we?" Paine said.

Vlota made no immediate response. To say that she lacked faith in Paine's sincerity would have been to understate the case enormously.

"It's a trick!" she returned.

"It's not a *trick!*" Paine said heatedly. "Call it a problem of etiquette for me, if you like. You Albanians have at least *heard* of etiquette, haven't you?"

Vlota's response was another superheated stream of curses in her native tongue. No translation was required for either Paine or Schwinn to grasp the basic drift of her reply.

"If you want to die right here and right now, that's your privilege, but I'd rather kill you later, when I can do it without committing a faux pas, all right? The woman's nothing to me, but I'm still a guest here, after all." Preaching civilized behavior to an Albanian was about as productive as flirting with a nun, Paine realized, but as long as they were talking, they weren't shooting, and there was something to be said for that.

"One wrong move and she dies!" Vlota said,

finally pushing Schwinn before her toward the bedroom door.

"And so do you, Vlota. Don't forget," Paine replied as he backed cautiously out into the hall.

The progress of the trio through the apartment was accomplished at the pace of a paranoid snail. More than once, John Paine was certain they wouldn't make it. But finally Vlota had backed up to the front door, and was reaching with one hand behind her for the knob.

"The next time we meet, you won't live to tell about it," she assured him.

"Talk's still awful cheap, isn't it?" Paine responded, with the .357 still aimed between the frightened eyes of the woman whose attire seemed so inappropriate for the encounter. "Careful now! Don't try anything frisky at the last moment!"

To his relief, Vlota didn't. She merely snarled a few more choice Albanian observations as she eased her lithe body through the door.

Then she slammed it behind her, and she was gone.

"Thank you, God," Schwinn gasped as Paine hurried to her to lead her away from the door ...just in case.

"I was wrong," Schwinn said a few minutes later when she'd had sufficient time to regain her composure and don a floor-length fuzzy blue robe. "You're not dashing and exciting."

She was looking at Paine with an expression far different from any she had directed at him before.

And well she should, he thought. She'd just

been forced to swallow a far larger helping of the brutal truth than most people ever had to choke down in the course of a lifetime. In his experience, no one ever did so without developing a severe case of existential indigestion, some of which had been known to last for years.

"You're right," he replied gently, "I'm not."

"You're more animal than man," Constance said without noticeable inflection. A kind of shock was setting in. Her about-to-be ex-lover could tell.

"Not really," Paine said, "that's a common misconception. Actually, man puts every beast I can think of to shame when it comes to unrestrained savagery."

Schwinn went on as if his words had not registered. She seemed lost in an avalanche of altered perceptions that had just thundered down on her with enormous weight and incredible speed.

"There's something terribly wrong with you," she said. "You're like androids, you and that murderous bitch. You've both been programmed to stalk and kill, and that's the only thing that matters to you. That's what she meant when she called you a monster, isn't it?"

"More or less," Paine replied. He was seated at the far end of the couch facing her. No cozy love seat for the two of them anymore. "As you surmise, Vlota is in no position to be hurling hyperbole about homicide. Between the two of us, she'd fit more neatly into a freak show than I would. For what it's worth." It was embarrassing to him to find himself indulging in the sort of sleazy self-justification that he most despised. Sitting still for the woman's open display of revulsion wasn't his idea of a great party, either. But Paine felt obligated to participate, having very nearly gotten Schwinn killed for no greater crime than joining him for a few acrobatic tumbles in the hay.

"You don't belong among normal people," she continued in that same flat, analytic voice. "Not *you*, and not that *creature* that just left. You belong out in the wild somewhere, someplace where you can tear each other apart without doing decent people any harm."

Paine was tempted to point out that he had said as much to Vlota only a few minutes before, but instead he said, "I had to say what I said ...about you...about us...because it was the only way to keep her from killing you to get at me." He diplomatically neglected to add that it had also been the pure, unvarnished truth.

"Really?" The way she said it put as sharp an edge on the word as that of any blade he had ever used. The woman had a certain talent for assassination herself, albeit of a cooler, drier variety than the kind Paine specialized in.

"If I'd handled it any other way, you'd be dead now. She'd have pulled the trigger at the least sign of affection toward you. It was for your sake that I didn't show any," he said, the words tasting to him as putrid as humble pie always did.

"What kind of people are you, that you could act that way?" she asked bitterly.

"You saw what kind we are," he answered simply. There were many other things he could have said. He could have asked her what gave her the right to stand in judgment of him; could have inquired to what extent she had lived free from sin herself. Had she never lied? Never wished she had the courage or the madness it took to do violence to someone who had richly deserved it for a long time? Never committed any of the little murders and minor thefts of daily life while telling herself she had not really transgressed because, in one way or another, what she'd done was right?

He could have told her that those good, decent, ordinary folks whom she extolled weren't really so good, so decent, or so ordinary if you took the trouble to inspect them closely without the rose-tinted glasses on. No one was. Including Constance Schwinn. Humankind did, in fact, occupy a jungle in which continuous savagery was more the rule than the exception; a savagery in which everyone played their part, be it ever so polite and stealthy and small. People like Vlota and himself were simply the average member of the species writ large. Not a breed apart. Paragons of what homo sapiens were and would always be. They only did in fact what multitudes of their brethren did in fantasy.

The gap between the two might look comfortably wide to Schwinn, but from where Paine stood, they looked as close as lovers and as hotly joined.

"How awful," she said.

"How true," he returned.

She fumbled with a pack of cigarettes to extract a smoke, spilling half its contents over the surface of the coffee table in the process. The hand that held the lighter trembled as she touched the shivering flame to the tip of the cigarette that was pressed tightly between her lips.

"You knew what I was the moment you laid your eyes on me," Paine assured her, wearying of her tirade of self-righteous condemnation. "You simply assumed you'd find a way to dance with the devil without getting burned. Admit it, Constance."

"I was looking for *excitement, Neal*, not *insanity!*" she shot back at him.

"Are you really so sure?" he asked.

"Yes! As sure as I need to be," she said forcefully, but her blue eyes wandered away, as if they were reluctant to meet his scrutiny.

"Good," he said, "I'm glad you're sure."

When the silence became oppressive between them, he said, "Are you through?"

"In more ways than one," she replied. "I think you should go."

"Yes. That thought had occurred to me, too," he said as he slowly stood up.

When he looked back one last time on his way out, Constance Schwinn was nowhere to be seen.

14

It was oppressively hot on Sunday afternoon when Cunningham took the jaunt down the freeway to the car wash that he always used. The surveillance team stayed close behind him all the way. The two agents assigned to him for the weekend looked bored, as if they would much prefer being at the beach to following Cunningham on his round of weekend chores.

It was good that they were bored, Cunningham knew. Because an indifferent observer was one who missed things. Perhaps only small things, but often, minor mistakes were all that was required. He had run them around throughout the morning for the express purpose of wearing them down. Starting shortly after he found the message in the dead-drop near his home.

Cunningham and Paine had chosen it long before, an insignificant breach in a stone fence next to a path in a small park a few blocks away. It was so situated that Cunningham could check it easily as he passed on one of the early morning rolls he was known to enjoy on the weekends. Loading the drop or unloading it called for no more than a brief pause beside the fence and a casual motion of the hand. Since Paine's return from Europe, the two friends had agreed that Cunningham would check the drop as often as possible without drawing suspicion.

Sunday morning's message had come as a relief. Paine had been out of touch for too long. Cunningham didn't like not knowing where his friend was or what his next move would be. Cunningham was too deeply involved to relish being left in the dark anymore. There was too much at stake. For him. For Paine. For everyone.

The line at the car wash was short when he turned off the street. Apparently the men on his tail weren't the only ones who viewed it as a good time to flee the suburban sprawl. As soon as he pulled his vehicle into position, one of the bare-chested Puerto Rican youths sauntered over to him for payment and the usual handsome tip that had endeared Cunningham to the entire crew.

"How you doing, man?" The wiry teenager flashed a brilliant smile and tossed in a wink with a slight nod to accompany it. The kid was good at saying things without saying them. Cunningham assumed that wherever the kid came from, children were well on their way to slick before they could handle trips to the bathroom by themselves.

"I'm doing great, Jesus, and you?" Cunningham responded, smiling, and paying attention to the boy's eyes.

"Couldn't be better, man. Now that you're

here. Business is good, you know?" Jesus kept the nod going as he glanced at the street behind Cunningham with eyes far older than his sixteen years. "Those feds goin' to get a wash, too? Or maybe they're just here to watch." He was staring at the government sedan that had pulled to the curb moments after Cunningham drove in.

Cunningham chuckled, impressed by the ease with which the youth had spotted his escort. Jesus might have trouble with spelling and multiplication, but identifying any "heat" in the vicinity was a subject at which he and the ghetto kids he worked with universally excelled.

"I imagine they'll just watch. That's what they're paid to do," Cunningham said.

"That's cool," Jesus said. "And you'll be cool, too. As long as you keep your air conditioner going when you're inside." He knew from past experience that Cunningham preferred to remain in the car to avoid the hassle of moving his crippled body and the chair back and forth. The slow, conveyor-driven trip down the enclosed length of the machine, with all its spinning brushes and hissing sprays, only took a few minutes. And the triple amputee never found the somewhat claustrophobic journey to be an unpleasant experience. He enjoyed it, in fact. It reminded him of one of the Tunnel of Love rides at some of the old amusement parks, with the pounding water, the gloom, and the temporary sense of complete isolation.

He was knowledgeable enough, too, to recognize the similarity between the car wash and the womb. Far be it from him to be any less subject to such Freudian blasts from the past than anyone else.

"Maybe I'll go mess with them a little bit while you're goin' through." Jesus's smile had a nasty twist to it when he said it. "Them feds got something up their butts, you know?"

"So I've heard," Kevin replied. They exchanged an amused glance at that. Jesus was not ignorant of the fact that Cunningham was some kind of fed, too. He had, however, granted him a special dispensation on the basis of his handicap and his tips.

"They figure their stuff don't smell. Like they was some kind of supercops. But you step on their dicks and they'll squeal like any other pig," Jesus said.

"You got a real way with words, Jesus," Cunningham said with a grimace.

"I know it, man. We been havin' a little trouble with the machine today," Jesus said as he backed away, watching the tail from the corner of his eye. "So don't panic if you get stuck in there for a while, all right?"

"I'll do all I can to remain calm," Cunningham returned as he rolled the window back up to the top.

The two exchanged one last quick look before Jesus turned and strolled toward the government car. Cunningham shifted into drive and eased ahead toward the mouth of the machine that was busy consuming the vehicle in front of the one in front of him. He glanced up at the mirror and smiled.

Jesus had acquired a sprayer and a rag on his way to the curb. As soon as he reached the surveillance sedan, he went to work, without troubling to consult them on whether his services were required. The agent riding shotgun opened his window and shouted something at the Puerto Rican youth that probably wasn't encouragement, from the nature of the expression on the man's face. Jesus ignored him, concentrating on the task of cleaning their windshield and managing to stretch himself prone across it as he did.

When the agent emerged from the car, convinced that nothing less than the direct approach would have any influence on the youth, Jesus slithered lithely across the hood and went to work on the windshield on the driver's side.

Cunningham moved ahead again after the next car was swallowed by the machine. When he checked the mirror again, another young member of the car wash crew had joined Jesus in baiting the surveillance team. Like the pack animals that they were, they darted in and out, taunting both men, but always staying just out of reach. Another lean and swarthy teenager jogged over to partake of the amusement moments before Cunningham's car was seized by the conveyor and dragged into the frothing tunnel before him.

Then all the windows were obscured by the water and the detergent and the whirling plastic brooms that flailed over them. Seconds later, the passenger door opened and John Paine plunged inside, dripping and flecked with foam.

"That's okay. I don't want the interior cleaned today," Cunningham said to his friend with a smile.

"Lucky for you," Paine replied, using his right index finger to squeegee the water from his broad forehead. "Because I don't want to clean it."

"How did you get Jesus and the gang organized to pull this operation off on such short notice?" Cunningham asked.

"By applying my profound understanding of developmental psychology, minority group sociology, and capitalism as practiced in the counterculture," Paine answered, drying the palms of both hands on his jeans.

"Which means... without all the organic fertilizer?" Cunningham inquired with elevated brows.

"I gave them the other half of these," Paine said, plucking the stubs of several hundred-dollar bills from his pocket, "and told them they could collect the mates when the job was successfully completed. I don't know why slum kids get such a bad rap these days. They're solid as a rock if you speak in terms they can understand."

"How did you explain the purpose of our meeting?" Cunningham asked.

"I didn't. Silence is another thing such youngsters understand quite well." As Paine concluded, the conveyor abruptly stopped. "I told them we only need five minutes without interruptions. In the meantime they'll be keeping your escort intensely occupied."

"So I noticed," Cunningham said with a grin.

"Your life is in serious danger, Kevin. I found out yesterday. From the horse's mouth, you might say," Paine said, with a voice turned suddenly serious. As quickly as possible he filled Cunningham in on his confrontation with Martina Vlota.

"Maybe I should thank my lucky stars I've got a close tail on me right now," Cunningham said.

"I wouldn't take much comfort from them if I were you," Paine said. "Those JDs are out there making monkeys of those characters right now, and Vlota is light-years beyond them when it comes to that sort of thing. Remember, she wasted two Bureau agents in the midst of a full-fledged police assault, then strolled away without anyone so much as laying a glove on her. If she wants you bad enough, she'll find a way to get to you. Believe it. You may find yourself having to deal with her yourself."

"Did she mention me specifically?" Cunningham's voice was taut with unease.

"No, but she didn't have to. She's out to destroy me and anyone close to me. That's a plan of attack that includes you by definition, unfortunately," Paine said.

"Don't worry about me, John. I can take care of myself. It's *your* future that really concerns me," Cunningham said.

"That makes two of us," Paine replied.

"Where do you go from here? Where will you stay? What will you do?" Cunningham said.

Paine told him.

"How about those codes? Have you found a way to get at them?" Paine asked.

"No, but frankly, the way things stand, I don't think you'll be needing them," Cunningham said.

"Oh? How's that?" Paine replied.

"That scare you threw into Rafferty worked like a charm," Cunningham said. "Ever since that morning, he's been calling people in to question them, and the scuttlebutt is that he's launched a massive background investigation of everyone in the Company who so much as said 'Good morning' once to Wilson. I assume you included a note in the surprise package you left for him."

"That's right, and apparently it had its intended effect," Paine replied. Then he shared with his friend the essence of the message. "I hope you're right. If so, then Rafferty will be doing my work for me. He's a good man, sharp and thorough. If anyone can be relied on to do justice, it should be him." Paine checked his watch. It told him that their time was about to run out.

"So you think if he looks close enough at all the people who could have gotten to Wilson, eventually he will turn up evidence that will establish a connection between the mole and whoever it is who's running him?" Cunningham asked.

"Exactly," Paine said.

"Sounds good. There's only one problem I can see," Cunningham said.

"Fire away. I love problems," Paine said.

"What if Rafferty is the mole?" Cunningham asked.

"Then I just screwed the pooch, didn't I?" Paine replied, turning toward the door.

"It's hard to know who to trust, isn't it?" Cunningham said.

"It always has been, partner. It always has been."

With that, Paine left Kevin Cunningham to take another bath.

15

Godunov was already seated at one of the little tables in the small outside garden when Paine arrived. This came as no surprise to the American agent, who knew his Soviet counterpart to be both punctual and professional in all things. The two longtime adversaries had chosen Puglia for its reliably noisy crowd, not its low-priced fine cuisine. The landmark on Hester Street in Little Italy was the kind of place where a wanted man could blend in; where councils of war were conducted over veal and ziti by men who wished to be ignored and were treated accordingly.

Mikhail Nikita Godunov was GRU, military intelligence. Paine thought the GRU bore the same relationship to the KGB that muggers bore to con artists. Both were after the same thing, but one believed in taking it by force; the other, in seducing their target into giving it to them.

The two violent men had faced one another repeatedly over the years; had come close to terminating one another more than once, but, as luck would have it, both had lived to recall every confrontation. The result had been a slowly accumulating respect and empathy that had finally, at some point neither could identify, matured into a solid friendship.

As the common wisdom would have it, and as Godunov and Paine knew to be true, every agent was more akin to every other agent, regardless of which nation they called home, than they were to the upper echelons of the service from which their fellow countrymen issued them commands. The similarities of experience, philosophy, and inclination that bound such men were far more substantial than the allegiances they shared with their managers.

Thus, it was not uncommon for such "enemies" to feel more warmth for one another than they ever felt for their superiors. So it was with Godunov and Paine, grizzled gladiators for their respective opposing systems. Neither was it unusual for the two of them to confer when one found himself faced with a particularly harrowing situation. They had even functioned briefly as a team twice before when one or both were facing a common enemy.

Paine had contacted Godunov at the Soviet Embassy in New York, where he was attached to the office of maritime affairs. It was one of those transparent covers in vogue in the game which amounted to nothing more than the refusal on the part of the employer to admit that a given individual did what everyone knew beyond any shadow of a doubt that he did.

He had been pleased and relieved to hear from

Paine. Godunov had learned of his friend's peril early on. In the meantime he had given Paine's rogue status much thought, wondering how he might be able to be of assistance, speculating on what profit might be made from the CIA fiasco.

"How good to see you, John. It has been too long," Godunov said, rising as Paine approached the table. Despite having been born and raised in Leningrad, when he spoke English, he did so with a distinctly British accent. The four years he'd spent perfecting his grasp of the language and pursuing a degree at Oxford had left their indelible mark on his speech.

"Indeed it has, Nikki. I see you haven't developed a taste for grubbies since we last met," Paine said. The two had fallen easily into a ritual of remarking on the other's taste in clothes, or lack thereof, whenever they got together. The custom stemmed from the polar opposition of their styles of dress. Paine preferred to go casual, as on this occasion, believing the less effort you put into your appearance, the more likely it was to go unnoticed. Godunov, on the other hand, was willing, if not eager, to draw attention to his ramrod deportment, graceful mannerisms, and elegant, upper-class style of dress. In Paine's opinion, Godunov was so vain that it worked to his advantage. Though eyes might be drawn his way, the last thing they would take him for was a spy. Or a killer. The long, thick gray hair that swept back over his head to lap over his collar brought to mind a symphony conductor. The tightly trimmed mustache and beard were those of an executive. The tailored, obviously expensive, pinstriped suit was the kind of subdued statement of money and power favored by the most successful trial lawyers. Paine knew that Godunov was the only GRU operative who was more likely to be taken for an investment banker than what he was.

Which, of course, served to make him all the more dangerous and effective.

"Better death before dishonor, John. And you haven't lost your weakness for impersonating a tramp, either. Isn't it comforting how we manage to remain true to ourselves, each in his own way, over the years?" Godunov extended his hand for a firm shake, then waited for Paine to take his seat before he returned to his.

"I haven't found that or anything else comforting in recent weeks, Nikki. As I'm sure you know," Paine responded. He could tell from the serpentine set of Godunov's knowing eyes that the GRU man was well informed as to the depth of his distress.

"Ah, yes. You've been very much the hot topic around the office lately. Could it be you had more in mind this evening that idle social chatter? Perhaps a few telling questions to the oracle of espionage?" Godunov lifted both the eyebrow and the corner of his mouth on the right side of his face. Anyone who did not know how cunning and heartless the man was might have found the expression silly. "I'm having cappuccino. Would you care for a cup before dinner?" Godunov asked. He was fingering the stainless steel expansion band of his Rolex as he watched

Paine, sliding it caressingly in and out of the French cuff of his rose silk shirt.

"Yes, thanks. Cappuccino will do fine," Paine said.

Godunov nodded to the waiter, whose attention had never strayed far from their table. The handsome young Italian lad knew a heavy tipper when he saw one. He was there in seconds.

"Cappuccino for my friend, please," Godunov said. He spoke quietly, but his voice possessed a resonant edge nonetheless. "And as to dinner..." He glanced at Paine by way of inquiry, and the American nodded his assent. "We will leave the choice to your commendable discretion. Something light and interesting if you will." Godunov dismissed the youth with a remark in Italian that Paine did not catch, but assumed was both amusing and complimentary, from the expression on the waiter's face as he hurried toward the kitchen.

The two men lighted cigarettes before the youth returned with the cup of steaming, caramel-colored brew for Paine.

"I could use a few state secrets if you have any you'd care to share with me," Paine said, eyeing Godunov over the rim of the cup as he savored its aroma. The bounds of secrecy was another subject they made light of whenever they met. They did so because each knew he was incapable of violating those inbred limits, even had he wanted to do so, no matter how close their friendship might be.

"I have some that might not be common knowledge quite yet. I don't know that they'd interest you, though. They surely don't interest me much," Godunov said.

"I'm dying to know if Moscow is running whoever is behind this problem I'm having with the Company," Paine said.

"So I am told," Godunov replied, tapping the ash from his Caporale into the ashtray between them. "If the KGB *is* behind it, it looks like they may have done something right for a change."

There was no more love lost between the GRU and the KGB than there was between the CIA and the FBI. It was the nature of the business that the various branches of a nation's security apparatus had less affection for one another than they had for their counterparts on the other side.

"Do you recall Martina Vlota?" Paine inquired.

"Martina... Vlota." Godunov stared up at the ceiling as he appeared to sort through his files for the name. After a few seconds he shook his head. "No, I don't believe I do."

"She's Albanian," Paine added.

"Good Lord!" Godunov sighed with an expression of profound chagrin. "Tell me, please, that circus act has not decided to make a stop in this fair town."

"I wish I could, but she is here, and most definitely out of sorts," Paine said. Then he proceeded to sketch the recent encounter with the woman for his friend.

"How distasteful. When will they ascend from that primitive darkness in which they dwell? She probably pursues her vendetta with the good wishes of whatever cretins she answers to," Godunov said.

"More than likely, yes," Paine agreed.

"So you're not only locked out in the cold, but you have a jackal out there with you. Life can be so unfair at times, can't it, John?" Godunov grinned and seemed on the verge of breaking into a chuckle.

"May you fall victim to the next purge of those who dine with the opposition," Paine said with an amiable wink.

"Hadn't you heard? We're above that sort of thing now. The new age has dawned with *glasnost* and *perestroika* for everyone," Godunov said. An ironic twinkle came to his eyes as he lifted his cup in a toast.

"No more Siberian gulags if you're late for work?" Paine inquired.

"They're turning them all into ski resorts, John. You have my word on it," Godunov said.

"But not for people like you and me, Nikki. They'll always have something special reserved for us," Paine said.

"They are going to kill you, John. We both know that, don't we?" Godunov looked into Paine's eyes as he butted the pungent French cigarette carefully into extinction.

"We both know they're giving it their best shot," Paine replied. "Thus far I'm way ahead on points."

"Ah, you Americans! Forever the bright-eyed optimists. I am touched. Reality has never been a problem for you, has it?" Godunov clasped his hands beneath his chin and studied his friend like an intriguing museum exhibit.

"Not like it has for you commies, no. You've got a point there, Nikki. We're so goofy, we've been running the whole planet for half a century," Paine rejoined. The merits of their respective systems was another subject over which the two liked to spar.

"Running it into the ground, some might say," Godunov said.

"Not as far into the ground as some of your most memorable achievements...like Uzbekistan," Paine vollied.

"The Philippines?" Godunov wondered.

"Lithuania," Paine said.

"Nicaragua," Godunov parried in perfect Spanish.

"Cuba," Paine said.

"Panama," Godunov replied.

"Afghanistan," Paine said with a bow of false admiration.

"Vietnam," Godunov whispered.

"South Africa," Paine said confidently.

"South Africa?" Godunov's brow furrowed. He glanced aside thoughtfully. "Are we responsible for all that, too?"

"Not to my knowledge. That was a curve ball," Paine said.

Godunov sighed. "God, that's a relief! All we need is apartheid to answer for along with everything else. Are you considering defecting, by the way?" The Soviet spy knew how to put one over the plate low and slow himself.

"I don't even speak Russian, Nikki. You know that," Paine replied.

"You could learn. It's easier to master than

resurrection, I imagine." Godunov waved for refills for their cappuccinos before looking back to Paine. "Your government doesn't love you anymore, John. You have become a painful embarrassment. Such problems are always handled by your employer in the same way they are handled by mine."

Paine said nothing. He didn't need to. Both knew what Godunov said was true.

"I will tell you something I shouldn't, John," Godunov said, then paused. He might have been considering whether he was courting the same fate as Paine. "Men like you and I..." He paused again, choosing his words. "Who can we count on besides each other? Our *friends* are more to be feared than our enemies, are they not?"

"Better the devil you know..." Paine replied.

"Exactly," Godunov said.

"Don't put yourself at risk for me, Nikki. You don't owe me," Paine said.

Godunov raised one hand in an elegant gesture of dismissal. "It's not for you. It's for myself. Everything I do, I do for me."

"All right," Paine replied. He could accept that premise readily. In their profession, those who did not answer, ultimately, to themselves alone were the rarest members of an endangered species.

"Your people have been inquiring as to the availability of various contract agents. It seems you have convinced them none of the standard measures will suffice," Godunov said.

"I'm surprised they waited this long," Paine replied.

"This is no more than hearsay, but I believe they have found someone. One of the best. Does this change your opinion on relocation?" Godunov leaned back in his chair, watching Paine, adjusting his tie automatically with one hand. "There are some ideal locations on the Black Sea where a man could retire and devote himself to his memoirs. I'd be more than happy to show you around."

"I'll bet you would. Like a prize trout. Do you know who took the contract?" Paine asked.

"No. I'm afraid not, but does it matter? They are all so much alike. He will be an obsessive who will not quit until one of you is dead. He could find you without help. But, as you know, he won't have to," Godunov said.

"Because the mole will be doing all he can to help out," Paine said, completing the thought for him.

Godunov shrugged his reply.

"If you're so eager to help me survive, why don't you tell me who the mole is? With his head to show people, I'm likely to be viewed in a far different light." Paine's eyes moved from Godunov to sweep the garden around them. The door that led to the adjoining restaurant interior was never out of his sight. As much as he enjoyed Little Italy, he could never pay a visit without recalling the occasional assassinations that took place there. Assassinations of dangerous men who'd mistakenly believed they could threaten the security of certain other dangerous men and get away with it.

"To even admit that I know a mole exists in the Company would mean crossing the line between friendship and treason, as you know. And, with all due respect, I don't like you enough to betray my country for you." Godunov lit another cigarette as he spoke.

"That makes two of us," Paine said.

"Just so. Touché. I will tell you this, however. We are not unfamiliar with such rodents where I come from, either. You have done your best to make certain of that, I am sure," Godunov said with a bleak smile.

"One does what one can," Paine said.

"In my experience, it is always the one everyone knows it cannot be. Someone who is above suspicion. Their position will be one of importance, but not too large so they can go about their work of deception unobserved. To be a mole means to lie with your every breath. To be a Judas who lives on the love of those he destroys. You will trust him with your life, offer him your daughter's hand. If a woman, she will be a natural mother to all, the wife every man craves, but with, perhaps, a naughty promise in her eyes to assure you she is not a good girl all the time, thereby making you want her all the more. They are always like this. They are the best. The rest of us are no more than fools at their feet," Godunov said.

He crossed one knee over the other and folded his arms as if to signal that the sermon was concluded.

"I really appreciate the encouragement, Nikki. Up to now I was thinking I was screwed," Paine said acridly.

"You are, John. I would be, too, in your position," Godunov said.

Just then the waiter arrived with a tray of steaming plates of pasta, mussels, and prawns.

"Excellent!" Godunov exclaimed. "You did very well. We'll have two carafes of this." With one finger he indicated a Neapolitan wine on the list that he favored.

"Make that one carafe," Paine said to the waiter.

"Ah, yes. My apologies. My friend is in training." Godunov continued looking at Paine as he spoke.

"Football?" the waiter guessed, judging from John Paine's build.

"No. He's a runner, actually," Godunov answered for Paine. "He hopes to do well in the Langley Marathon, don't you, John?"

"Best of luck, sir," the waiter said with a smile before he went for the wine.

"You making sure the condemned man enjoys his last meal?" Paine asked, surveying the assortment of delectables spread out before him.

"Something like that. A token of my esteem, and not the last one if another satisfactory opportunity arises," Godunov said as he savored the scent of a mussel before he consumed it.

"Why not just tell me what I want to know, and get it off your chest?" Paine asked.

"Why should I? Stop acting like you're not having fun. I know you are. This disaster is tailor-made for a man like you. What more could a born killer ask than to be surrounded by targets?" Godunov asked before he attacked his fettuccini.

"Waking up one morning to discover you'd

turned into Hugh Hefner," Paine answered succinctly.

"Damn straight, old boy!" Godunov responded.

"In his place, I'd want to be," Paine said.

16

The hotel was located on Avenue "B" in Alphabet City on Manhattan's notorious Lower East Side. Some of its rooms rented by the hour. Credit cards and checks were good only for a few meager laughs. No questions were asked of the customers, who consisted mainly of whores, hypes, and fugitives who were too busy watching their backs to worry about what might be scurrying around at their feet.

The young toughs who lounged by the entrances to the building, both front and rear, did not look like the sentries that they were. They were typically sporting ponytails and tattoos, wearing muscle shirts, baggy pants, and sandals. Their guns and knives were concealed, and they seemed to care only for their bottled beer and blaring boom boxes. But they watched every inch of the graffiti-laden landscape around them, which they claimed as their turf and defended against all invasions, including the occasional cautious sortie by the NYPD.

The guard assignment was only temporary

employment for them, but that was the only kind of job they were known to accept. It paid well... cash in advance, and the man who had recruited them was one whose simple needs and dark nature they could admire and understand. This recent resident of the hotel was twice their age, but twice their size, as well, and hard as oak. He'd said that there wasn't much to do: just roust anyone they didn't know, refuse to let strangers pass without a frisk, and generally ensure him a few days and nights of peace and quiet.

He'd been blunt with them about the only real drawback to the arrangement, the likelihood that they would die young if they got between him and his enemies. They had been as unmoved by that possibility as he had expected.

When the four gang members stationed by the door that opened on the alley behind the hotel saw the little man in the tattered trenchcoat approaching, they were unimpressed. His movements were halting and uncertain, as if he might be drunk or lost, or both. The coat alone, on such a steaming night, was proof enough that madness had overtaken him, as it had so many others in the vicinity. He wore a felt hat, as well, with a wide brim that was pulled low over his face.

"Hey! Check out the dwarf, man! Looks like he stole himself a tree!" The one of the quartet who spoke laughed with the rest at the odd contrast between the size of the bum and the size of the staff upon which he leaned his weight. The polished length of the straight rod extended several inches above his head. Its thickness was sufficient to fill the hand that grasped it. The man's other hand was clenched around the neck of an open bottle of Thunderbird wine.

They watched him weave slowly toward them, pausing between shuffling steps to raise the bottle long enough for a quick swig. The light in the littered corridor that divided the block was too dim for them to see him well until he reached the foot of the stoop on which they sat or stood.

"Hold it right there, *cabrón*! Nobody gets inside 'less we check them for weapons." The youth closest to the bum looked around at the others impishly, enjoying himself at the derelict's expense. "But maybe I give you a break if you share some of that wine with me, huh?" He extended his hand for the bottle, knowing the wino would guard it with his life.

"Maybe I'll give you a break, too," Samson said softly. Then he raised his head so the kid could see his face. As the thug stood temporarily frozen by the nightmare visage before him, Samson whipped the bottle down against the steps, shattering it. When his hand swept back up, it held only the neck and the jagged glass fangs that remained. He drove them into the guard's throat before the boy had time to react.

Minutes earlier, on the sidewalk near the hotel's front door, the three guards on duty there had found themselves facing a vision of a far more palatable kind. A cab had pulled over to the curb directly in front of them, and when its backdoor opened, the world's most perfect pair of legs had suddenly emerged. Their owner had perched at length on the seat, letting them look, as she dug through her purse in search of the fare.

She was dressed in a way that advertised her calling and the nature of the "house call" she was about to make: sheerest hose and high heels, short shorts, and a Spandex leotard that clung possessively to the dainty contours of her breasts. The way she moved was brazen, as flashy and provocative as her makeup and perfume.

As the taxi pulled away, she stood watching it for a moment with her back to them, with no other evident purpose than the desire to assure them that the view was equally good from both sides. Then she turned and strutted toward them, looking each in the eye as the distance between them closed.

"You got any samples for us tonight, mama?"

"You lucked out, baby! We like it close to the bone!"

"You gonna get in trouble, you keep walkin' like that!"

The three casually formed a line between the hooker and the door as each expressed his approval loud and clear. When she tried to pass between them, the homeboy in the middle used her left breast as a handle with which to shove her back a step. The blow she delivered to his wrist was hard and fast enough to hand him a shock. He was about to give her the back of his fist across the face when the savage look in her eyes persuaded him to exercise self-restraint. She was a hard one. As hard, probably, as he was himself, regardless of her sex and the way she sold it for a living. He had seen her kind before. He knew whores like her specialized in johns who would pay such a she-devil to give them what they deserved.

"Get out of my way. I have someone waiting for me inside," she said.

The one in the middle just smiled at her lean, frigid face as his companions silently looked her over, making individual estimates as to what her top speed might be.

"What's your hurry? You afraid he's gonna do it by himself if you ain't on time?" The one on her left was handsome and muscular, and he knew it. He wasn't awed by her nasty act. In his world there were many women who came on cold as ice like that, but he knew there was always fire underneath. What he didn't know was how hot that fire might be. That was an ignorance from which he would not be suffering for very long.

Martina Vlota would see to that.

The cab and the Irma La Douce outfit were the window dressing she had chosen to get her inside Paine's "perimeter" without causing a stir. It was one thing to continue tracking him from a distance as she had done. Even that required great skill and circumspection. But to close in for the kill called for sly cunning of the highest order. The stalemate at the woman's apartment had convinced Vlota that Paine was capable of slipping through even the tightest noose. He required only the slightest warning to save himself. But she would not give him even that. All that was necessary was to bluff her way past the horny goons.

If necessary, she would gladly service all three if that would get her inside. She wouldn't be abused, but she would be balled if need be. They could paw and grope and prod whatever appealed to them. As long as it wasn't her purse.

Her purse, of course, was the first thing they wanted to examine, before they got on to the rest.

"What's in the bag, bitch?" the one on her right asked. Like his buddies, he had little trust to spare for the world at large, and none at all when it came to prostitutes. When he reached for it, Vlota forced an inviting smile onto her face as she swung the purse behind her to clutch it against her butt with both hands.

"Rubbers and douche and breath mints, honey. You know how it is, right? Why don't we be nice to each other instead of hassling like this? I can be very nice when I want to be," she crooned. Vlota snaked her tongue over her lower lip, pulled her shoulders together to showcase her nubby breasts, cocked one leg to accentuate the symmetry of her thigh.

From the lewd grins on the three dark faces before her, Vlota assumed that the ploy was working. When they closed in around her, she didn't back away or resist. Their hands moved over her with crude expertness, grasping this and stroking that, while she gave them a practiced pantomime of passion.

When her leotard was jerked down to her narrow waist, baring her dusky, childish chest, she was sure she had them. Then the hand that was squeezing one of the hard little hemispheres of her derriere went for the purse, grasping it long enough to learn that it concealed the tool of a rather different and more deadly trade.

"Rubbers, huh?" were the last words of the one who made the discovery.

Before he could alert his friends, Vlota twisted free of them with unexpected strength. She was reaching into the purse as she lurched away, slipping her hand around the grip of the H & K nine-millimeter automatic. She knew instinctively there was no more possibility for stealth. Savage speed was all that remained. She released the purse to use both hands on the gun. Before it hit the ground, she fired point-blank into the face of the one on the left.

He was still on his way down when she did the same for the one in the middle. While part of her mind screamed that Paine was even then launching into action, another part was thrilling to the expression of helpless horror on Mr. Macho's face the instant before she pulled the trigger and erased it. The thunderclaps of the automatic were deafening, and could be heard for blocks. The guard who remained was backpedaling toward the entrance and fumbling for the .38 tucked into his pants at the small of his back when Vlota put her third shot precisely through his neck.

Then she was sprinting to the entrance with every ounce of her electric speed.

Samson unsheathed the wicked blade at the end of his staff with a single swift, hard jerk. Even as he did, he was swinging its other end up to slam into the ribs of the guard on his right. The youth was folding from the bone-breaking blow as Samson drove the point of the spear into the chest of the one nearest the door. No sooner had the dagger entered its full length than he yanked it free, pivoting the rod around to drive its butt into the solar plexus of the last one, who stood frozen by the sudden demonstration of bloody martial expertise.

First one, and then the other, Samson finished the two he had clubbed with a single, brutal thrust of the blade. He was dropping the staff and about to remove the coat that concealed the silenced Uzi slung over his shoulder when the shots rang out from the front of the hotel. He paused for a moment of consternation, unsure of what the gunfire portended, before he rushed inside.

John Paine hesitated in the third-floor hallway outside the door of his room with the Ingram machine pistol grasped securely in both hands. The shots had come from the street in front. Was it time to flee or time to fight? He didn't know, and would not commit himself until he did.

On the main floor Samson was striding down the hallway toward the front desk when an old man's head emerged from a door a few feet in front of him on his right. "What the hell?" the old man said, an instant before he was decapitated by a short, burping burst from the Uzi.

Samson saw Vlota pressing the muzzle of her automatic to the nose of the night clerk, encouraging him to share Paine's room number with her, seconds before she saw him. He hesitated before he fired, bemused by the spectacle.

The way the young woman was attired and the way she held the gun did not fit together. Before he could consider the matter further, Vlota spied him from the corner of her eye, swung the nine-millimeter in his direction, and squeezed off a round.

From where he stood two floors above, locked in the grip of indecision, Paine heard first another handgun blast, then the unmistakable coughing of a silenced submachine gun. That was all it took to help him make up his mind. There had been a day when he would hurl himself into a firefight with blood in his eye and a smile on his lips, but he was much older and a good deal wiser than he had been then.

Half a dozen long strides carried him to the stairs. Three at a time, he plunged upward, flight after flight, until he reached the exit onto the roof. He did not pause when the muggy night enveloped him, but dashed to the rampart where the structure and its neighbor met, vaulted it, and continued in that way until he reached the end of the block, where he cautiously descended a fire escape to the street below.

Behind him, Vlota and Samson did their best to kill each other, failed, and retreated, cursing at the sure knowledge that their wary quarry had already taken wing, back the way they had come...

To pick up the rogue agent's scent and, like the hellhounds they were, rabidly return to the chase.

SPECIAL PREVIEW

*Here are the
exciting opening scenes from*

ROGUE AGENT #4
Last Rites

Coming in August 1991!

John Paine dropped from the fire escape onto the sidewalk as lightly as any two hundred thirty pound man could. Behind him the nasty crackle of gunfire continued in the vicinity of the hotel. It was hardly an unusual sound in that portion of Manhattan, the Lower East Side, but even in that savage setting it was not likely to go unnoticed by the perpetual police presence for too long.

Knowing this, Paine did not linger. But once his feet hit the littered street, neither did he run. To run was to attract attention. Instead he strolled. Listening closely for even the slightest resonance of pursuit. Who had found him this time, and how? he wondered. There was no way for him to know. He could only hope that whoever they were they did not survive to carry on the chase. But if they did, he had a new identity in mind that should throw them off the scent. For a few days, at least. He needed time. Time to think. About the mole.

A traitor was hidden among the ranks of his

employer, the Central Intelligence Agency. Someone who had managed somehow to set in motion a chain of events that had driven John Paine out into the cold, branded as a renegade. A once-trusted field operative who must now die for the mortal sin of disobedience.

As he stepped lightly over the still form of a Hispanic male who was either taking a break or dead, Paine wondered how many people were dedicated to his demise, how many more killers would come after him. A cruiser shrieked past, headed for the cockroach farm he'd just fled, and Paine vowed that he would be ready for them, regardless of their number, regardless of how good they might be. He didn't consider himself the best, but there were some in the trade who viewed him that way.

He knew that humility was the most valuable survival skill he possessed, over the long haul. As in most other sectors of life, pride directly preceded a fall. And when killing was your business, the falls were usually the kind from which you didn't recover. So Paine was content to leave the pleasures of arrogance to the competition. To his way of thinking, "modest and breathing" was much preferable to "vain and not."

While Paine put distance between himself and the recent near-miss, the NYPD was busy learning how much trouble a pair of career cutthroats could be...

When Samson slaughtered his way through Paine's recruited sentries in the alley behind the hotel, he had done it as quietly as only a truly gifted butcher could. He was a virtuoso with a spear at close quarters. The smirking delinquents who'd laughed at his diminutive size had been no more than sperms and eggs in strangers when the merc had begun the study of kendo.

Samson had nearly chosen a samurai sword to postpone the gunplay, instead of the spear. In the end, however, he'd decided it was too obvious. That was a shame. With it he could have made the final moments of the punks ever so much more interesting than they had been. In the proper hands, such a weapon was transformed into a great Cuisinart, a whizzing slice-and-dice machine that could disassemble an individual so swiftly that the victim would have no time to appreciate the process.

All of his stealth had been rendered pointless, however, when the shots reverberated in the street on the hotel's other side. Then Samson had known he was running out of time as he seized the silenced Uzi that lay concealed beneath his Goodwill overcoat. For a moment he'd considered scrubbing the mission, blowing it off as one of those times when a good plan was ruined by unforeseeable events.

But instinct had urged him to proceed. So he did. Only to be confronted moments later by a wiry, boyish bitch in hot pants who handled a Heckler & Koch P7 nine-millimeter automatic far better than any woman should who made a living by turning big ones into little ones. In the instant before she'd swung the muzzle toward him, Samson had failed to recognize the face, but the form was only too familiar. The practiced, predatory way she moved had "professional" inscribed into every gesture. Somehow the two of them had managed a masterpiece of bad timing, making their separate, independent attempts on Paine at precisely the same moment.

Samson found their accidental folly amusing, but the humorless "hooker" forced him to dive for cover before he could share the joke with her and put a few chunky slugs into her lithe physique.

As Samson assumed, Martina Vlota found his sudden appearance less than hilarious. Like him, a mere glimpse was enough to recognize another of her kind. Even as she fired at the gnome's darting shape, she cursed the gridlock of enemies the bastard Paine seemed to attract. She wanted the sadistic brute to herself. She had earned that much after the horror he had put her through. But the army of all the others who hungered for his bones seemed committed to forcing her to share with them the cold flavor of her revenge.

As she vented her frustration with each accurate shot at Samson, Vlota clung to the desperate hope that her quarry would choose to fight, not flee. But as the minutes passed since she'd wasted the horny goons guarding the front door, she was forced to acknowledge that the wily rogue had opted for discretion instead.

Though the understanding came as a disappointment, it was hardly a surprise. It was Paine's reflexive caution that had been Vlota's undoing at the start. There'd been no apparent reason for him to wear the Kevlar on that balmy night when she'd shot him in the midst of the Adriatic Sea. She had successfully camouflaged herself among the crew, passing herself off as a male steward as only an androgynous sexual chameleon could.

So Vlota had assumed he wasn't wearing it. When he collapsed onto the deck she had been certain of her triumph, confident that she could hover over him to deliver the makesure shot and savor it as her reward for a job well-done. And it was then that Paine had erupted into life beneath her, lifting her with his brawny legs and kicking her like so much flailing garbage, over the side, to eventual death by drowning in the rolling salty wilderness below.

But Vlota had been too strong and a little too lucky to die, and she had a ravenous appetite for revenge that helped to keep her afloat.

Now another chance for repayment had been blown, and, she knew, the ever-mounting siren screams meant that her chances of escape were dwindling by the second. And Paine was slipping farther away, his trail growing cold and losing its scent.

Samson's train of thought, as he returned her fire with repeated, short, muffled bursts, was very much the same. He wanted her dead as badly as she craved the same for him, but first things first. It wouldn't do to let one's priorities get confused.

Therefore, when he saw Vlota backing toward the front entrance, he let her go, knowing she still stood a strong chance of being killed by the arriving police. On the other hand, so did he. As adept at and inclined toward murder as he might be, Samson knew he was not supernatural. He was a force of one. The NYPD, whatever skill they might lack, numbered in the thousands.

From the sound of the accumulating chorus of wails coming from every direction, it seemed as if half of them had decided to show up for the party.

Vlota had just emerged onto the hotel's front steps when the first blue-and-white made a wailing, skidding crash stop in the street. Without the purse, stashing the H & K was something of a challenge. Her body was spare, and the little she wore was hardly more than another layer of skin. She settled for stuffing the compact nine-millimeter between her stretchy waistband and her spine.

Then the Albanian assassin went into her act with a long, skull-piercing scream.

"He's killing everyone! Mary, mother of God! There's blood everywhere!" She staggered down the steps toward them, taking pains to keep her back close to the wall. Vlota pressed a hand to each side of her head, as if trying to contain the boiling hysteria within.

One of the two patrolmen who'd emerged from the cruiser advanced on the hotel entrance, waving the hooker out of the way, crouching with his gun held high and ready. He was buying her performance, but not completely. He'd been a cop in New York too long to assume that any prostitute was nonviolent.

Vlota crabbed sideways down the sidewalk, fearing that John Paine was surely long gone by then. As disturbing as she found the prospect of losing him, she knew she must concentrate for the moment on her escape. She must keep the victim act going until she was safely away. Then she would have to find him again. She thought she knew how she would do that; do it in a way that would hurt the man she loathed in more ways than one.

Vlota could hardly wait.

"Careful, Jimmy!" The partner who'd remained behind the opened door of the cruiser, covering the entrance with a sawed-off twelve-gauge pump, barked the warning as a score and more patrol cars arrived. Most took up positions in the street, but several crowded into the alley behind the building, as well.

As soon as the Albanian spotted a cruiser with a lone cop behind the wheel, she hurried over to it, hugging herself with both arms and whimpering convincingly. She had to force herself not to look behind her. That would seem suspicious, she thought. She would have to trust the luck that appeared to have deserted her recently. If a cop got behind her and saw the menacing silhouette riding her tail... she was finished.

But so was he. And as many of his pals as she could take with her before the end.

"Oh, Jesus, Officer! I'm so scared!" she said to him. He was young and handsome. Vlota noted the way his eyes dropped for an instant to her long, hard legs.

"What's going on in there?" he asked.

"There's a nut with a machine-gun. He's blowing everyone away. I don't know how I got out alive!" She loaded her voice and expression with all the vulnerable appeal she could muster.

"Why don't you get in the back. You'll be safer there." The officer reached over the seat to open the door for her.

"Sounds good to me," Vlota said. She hopped into the rear of the cruiser, pulling the door closed as soon as she had drawn her legs inside.

"It's a good thing you got out of there alive," the rookie said as he turned around on the seat to get a better look at her. "A good body is a terrible thing to waste."

"You like what you see?" she asked, reaching behind her back casually as his eyes visited various points of interest.

"You could say that, yeah," he replied.

When her hand reappeared grasping the stubby nine, the cop suddenly lost interest in everything but the bore.

"How about life? You like that, too?" Vlota inquired, keeping the automatic beneath the level of the window next to her, aiming at the point on the seat between the P7 and his heart.

It came too late, but the youth finally realized the woman was not what she seemed. "Sure do," he said evenly. "It's gotten to be a regular habit."

"Then get me out of here, and don't get cute while you're at it. We get stopped; you get shot ... several times. My word on it. Now turn around. Maybe if you're good you'll live to make a pass at someone who's impressed," Vlota said.

He did as he was told. "Consider this a cab."

"Don't worry. I do," she responded.

Samson was in the alley behind the hotel when cruisers sealed it off at both ends. He was too much the warrior not to consider blasting his way through them, at least briefly. Then common sense prevailed. He really stood to lose very little by surrendering. He had already made sure of that.

So when they saw him there and bellowed their commands, Samson reluctantly complied. He tossed the Uzi onto the grimy pavement where they could see it and followed it with the Python he was carrying as backup. Then he dropped to his knees, laced his fingers behind his head, and waited as a dozen blue suits approached him from both directions.

The first cop to draw near almost shot Samson when he got a good look at his face. It was a hellish reconstructed landscape that provoked violent reactions wherever it appeared.

"You twitch, and I'll make you uglier than you already are, pal," the cop said.

"Sticks and stones, Officer. Sticks and stones," Samson replied softly as the left side of his mouth twitched up to reveal his fine, white teeth.

"I think we need an exorcist," another cop said.

"You give *ugly* a whole new meaning, little dude." The third officer had picked up the Uzi and was aiming it at Samson's chest.

"Sort of what you do for *stupid*, right?" Samson replied with a dry chuckle.

"You have the right to remain silent..." one of them began, but Samson cut him off.

"Skip it, I'm a government agent," he said.

"Like hell you are," the one with the Uzi said with total disbelief.

"You could say that, but it's beside the point.

I have a document to show you, and a number for you to call. Then I will be on my way," Samson said.

And he assumed it would be that simple. But he was in New York City, where things did not always go according to plan.

So it was anything but simple.

GRITTY, SUSPENSEFUL NOVELS BY MASTER STORYTELLERS FROM AVON BOOKS

OUT ON THE CUTTING EDGE
by Lawrence Block
70993-7/$4.95 US/$5.95 Can

"Exceptional... A whale of a knockout punch to the solar plexus."
New York Daily News

FORCE OF NATURE
by Stephen Solomita
70949-X/$4.95 US/$5.95 Can

"Powerful and relentlessly engaging... Tension at a riveting peak" *Publishers Weekly*

A TWIST OF THE KNIFE
by Stephen Solomita
70997-X/$4.95 US/$5.95 Can

"A sizzler... Wambaugh and Caunitz had better look out"
Associated Press

BLACK CHERRY BLUES
by James Lee Burke
71204-0/$4.95 US/$5.95 Can

"Remarkable... A terrific story... The plot crackles with events and suspense... Not to be missed!"
Los Angeles Times Book Review

Buy these books at your local bookstore or use this coupon for ordering:

Mail to: Avon Books, Dept BP, Box 767, Rte 2, Dresden, TN 38225
Please send me the book(s) I have checked above.
☐ My check or money order—no cash or CODs please—for $_____ is enclosed
(please add $1.00 to cover postage and handling for each book ordered to a maximum of three dollars).
☐ Charge my VISA/MC Acct#_____ Exp Date_____
Phone No_____
I am ordering a minimum of two books (please add postage and handling charge of $2.00 plus 50 cents per title after the first two books to a maximum of six dollars). For faster service, call 1-800-762-0779. Residents of Tennessee, please call 1-800-633-1607. Prices and numbers are subject to change without notice. Please allow six to eight weeks for delivery.

Name _____
Address _____
City _____ State/Zip _____

Tough Guys 10/90

#1
HIS THIRD CONSECUTIVE NUMBER ONE BESTSELLER!

James Clavell's
WHIRLWIND

70312-2/$6.99 US/$7.99 CAN

From the author of *Shōgun* and *Noble House*—
the newest epic in the magnificent Asian Saga
is now in paperback!

"WHIRLWIND IS A CLASSIC—FOR OUR TIME!"
Chicago Sun-Times

WHIRLWIND

is the gripping epic of a world-shattering upheaval that alters the destiny of nations. Men and women barter for their very lives. Lovers struggle against heartbreaking odds. And an ancient land battles to survive as a new reign of terror closes in...

Buy these books at your local bookstore or use this coupon for ordering:

Mail to: Avon Books, Dept BP, Box 767, Rte 2, Dresden, TN 38225
Please send me the book(s) I have checked above.
☐ My check or money order—no cash or CODs please—for $_____ is enclosed (please add $1.00 to cover postage and handling for each book ordered to a maximum of three dollars).
☐ Charge my VISA/MC Acct# _____ Exp Date _____
Phone No _____ I am ordering a minimum of two books (please add postage and handling charge of $2.00 plus 50 cents per title after the first two books to a maximum of six dollars). For faster service, call 1-800-762-0779. Residents of Tennessee, please call 1-800-633-1607. Prices and numbers are subject to change without notice. Please allow six to eight weeks for delivery.

Name _____
Address _____
City _____ State/Zip _____

JCW 2/91

FROM PERSONAL JOURNALS TO BLACKLY HUMOROUS ACCOUNTS

VIETNAM

DISPATCHES, Michael Herr
01976-0/$4.50 US/$5.95 Can
"I believe it may be the best personal journal about war, any war, that any writer has ever accomplished."
—Robert Stone, *Chicago Tribune*

M, John Sack
69866-8/$3.95 US/$4.95 Can
"A gripping and honest account, compassionate and rich, colorful and blackly comic."
—*The New York Times*

ONE BUGLE, NO DRUMS, Charles Durden
69260-0/$4.95 US/$5.95 Can
"The funniest, ghastliest military scenes put to paper since Joseph Heller wrote *Catch-22*"
—*Newsweek*

AMERICAN BOYS, Steven Phillip Smith
67934-5/$4.50 US/$5.95 Can
"The best novel I've come across on the war in Vietnam"
—Norman Mailer

Buy these books at your local bookstore or use this coupon for ordering:

Mail to: Avon Books, Dept BP, Box 767, Rte 2, Dresden, TN 38225
Please send me the book(s) I have checked above.
☐ My check or money order—no cash or CODs please—for $_____ is enclosed
(please add $1.00 to cover postage and handling for each book ordered to a maximum of three dollars).
☐ Charge my VISA/MC Acct# _____ Exp Date _____
Phone No _____ I am ordering a minimum of two books (please add postage and handling charge of $2.00 plus 50 cents per title after the first two books to a maximum of six dollars). For faster service, call 1-800-762-0779. Residents of Tennessee, please call 1-800-633-1607. Prices and numbers are subject to change without notice. Please allow six to eight weeks for delivery.

Name _____
Address _____
City _____ State/Zip _____

Vietnam 5/90

STUART WOODS
The *New York Times* Bestselling Author

GRASS ROOTS
71169-9/$4.95 US/$5.95 Can

When the nation's most influential senator succumbs to a stroke, his brilliant chief aide runs in his stead, tackling scandal, the governor of Georgia and a white supremacist organization that would rather see him dead than in office.

Don't miss these other page-turners from Stuart Woods

WHITE CARGO   70783-7/$4.95 US/$5.95 Can
A father searches for his kidnapped daughter in the drug-soaked Colombian underworld.

DEEP LIE   70266-5/$4.95 US/$5.95 Can
At a secret Baltic submarine base, a renegade Soviet commander prepares a plan so outrageous that it just might work.

UNDER THE LAKE   70519-2/$4.50 US/$5.95 Can
CHIEFS   70347-5/$4.95 US/$5.95 Can
RUN BEFORE THE WIND
      70507-9/$4.95 US/$5.95 Can

Buy these books at your local bookstore or use this coupon for ordering:

Mail to: Avon Books, Dept BP, Box 767, Rte 2, Dresden, TN 38225
Please send me the book(s) I have checked above.
☐ My check or money order—no cash or CODs please—for $_____ is enclosed (please add $1.00 to cover postage and handling for each book ordered to a maximum of three dollars).
☐ Charge my VISA/MC Acct#_____ Exp Date _____
Phone No _____ I am ordering a minimum of two books (please add postage and handling charge of $2.00 plus 50 cents per title after the first two books to a maximum of six dollars). For faster service, call 1-800-762-0779. Residents of Tennessee, please call 1-800-633-1607. Prices and numbers are subject to change without notice. Please allow six to eight weeks for delivery.

Name_____
Address_____
City _____ State/Zip _____